MY LiFe
as a
Walrus
Whoopee
Cushion

BOOKS BY BILL MYERS

The Incredible Worlds of Wally McDoogle (20 books):

—*My Life As a Smashed Burrito with Extra Hot Sauce*
—*My Life As Alien Monster Bait*
—*My Life As a Broken Bungee Cord*
—*My Life As Crocodile Junk Food*
—*My Life As Dinosaur Dental Floss*
—*My Life As a Torpedo Test Target*
—*My Life As a Human Hockey Puck*
—*My Life As an Afterthought Astronaut*
—*My Life As Reindeer Road Kill*
—*My Life As a Toasted Time Traveler*
—*My Life As Polluted Pond Scum*
—*My Life As a Bigfoot Breath Mint*
—*My Life As a Blundering Ballerina*
—*My Life As a Screaming Skydiver*
—*My Life As a Human Hairball*
—*My Life As a Walrus Whoopee Cushion*
—*My Life As a Mixed-Up Millennium Bug*
—*My Life As a Beat-Up Basketball Backboard*
—*My Life As a Cowboy Cowpie*
—*My Life As Invisible Intestines with Intense Indigestion*

Other Series:

McGee and Me! (12 books)

Bloodhounds, Inc. (10 books)

Forbidden Doors (10 books)

Teen Nonfiction

Hot Topics, Tough Questions
Faith Encounter
Just Believe It

Picture Book

Baseball for Breakfast

www.Billmyers.com

#10—*My Life As a Toasted Time Traveler*
Wally travels back from the future to warn himself of an upcoming accident. But before he knows it, there are more Wallys running around than even Wally himself can handle. Catastrophes reach an all-time high as Wally tries to out-think God and re-write history. (ISBN 0-8499-3867-8)

#11—*My Life As Polluted Pond Scum*
This laugh-filled Wally disaster includes: a monster lurking in the depths of a mysterious lake . . . a glowing figure with powers to summon the creature to the shore . . . and one Wally McDoogle, who reluctantly stumbles upon the truth. Wally's entire town is in danger. He must race against the clock, his own fears, and learn to trust God before he has any chance of saving the day. (ISBN 0-8499-3875-9)

#12—*My Life As a Bigfoot Breath Mint*
Wally gets his big break to star with his uncle Max in the famous Fantasmo World stunt show. Unlike his father, whom Wally secretly suspects to be a major loser, Uncle Max is everything Wally longs to be . . . or so it appears. But Wally soon discovers the truth and learns who the real hero is in his life. (ISBN 0-8499-3876-7)

#13—*My Life As a Blundering Ballerina*
Wally agrees to switch places with Wall Street. Everyone is in on the act as the two try to survive seventy-two hours in each other's shoes and learn the importance of respecting other people. (ISBN 0-8499-4022-2)

#14—*My Life As a Screaming Skydiver*
Master of mayhem Wally turns a game of laser tag into international espionage. From the Swiss Alps to the African plains, Agent 00½th bumblingly employs such top-secret gizmos as rocket-powered toilet paper, exploding dental floss, and the ever-popular transformer tacos to stop the dreaded and super secret . . . Giggle Gun. (ISBN 0-8499-4023-0)

#15—*My Life As a Human Hairball*
When Wally and Wall Street visit a local laboratory, they are accidentally miniaturized and swallowed by some unknown

stranger. It is a race against the clock as they fly through various parts of the body in a desperate search for a way out while learning how wonderfully we're made. (ISBN 0-8499-4024-9)

#16—My Life As a Walrus Whoopee Cushion
Wally and his buddies, Opera and Wall Street, win the Gazillion Dollar Lotto! Everything is great, until they realize they lost the ticket at the zoo! Add some bungling bad guys, a zoo break-in, the release of all the animals, a SWAT team or two . . . and you have the usual McDoogle mayhem as Wally learns the dangers of greed. (ISBN 0-8499-4025-7)

#17—My Life As a Mixed-Up Millennium Bug
When Wally accidently fries the circuits of Ol' Betsy, his beloved laptop computer, suddenly whatever he types turns into reality! At 11:59, New Year's Eve, Wally tries retyping the truth into his computer—which shorts out every other computer in the world. By midnight, the entire universe has credited Wally's mishap to the MILLENNIUM BUG! Panic, chaos, and hilarity start the new century, thanks to our beloved boy blunder.
(ISBN 0-8499-4026-5)

#18—My Life As a Beat-Up Basketball Backboard
Ricko Slicko's Advertising Agency claims that they can turn the dorkiest human in the world into the most popular. And who better to prove this than our boy blunder, Wally McDoogle! Soon he has his own TV series and fans wearing glasses just like his. But when he tries to be a star athlete for his school basketball team, Wally finally learns that being popular isn't all it's cut out to be. (ISBN 0-8499-4027-3)

#19—My Life As a Cowboy Cowpie
Once again our part-time hero and full-time walking disaster finds himself smack dab in another misadventure. This time it's full of dude-ranch disasters, bungling broncobusters, and the world's biggest cow—well let's just say it's not a pretty picture (or a pleasant smelling one). Through it all, Wally learns the dangers of seeking revenge. (ISBN 0-8499-5990-X)

the incredible worlds of **Wally McDoogle**

MY LiFe
as a
Walrus
Whoopee
Cushion

B I L L   M Y E R S

Tommy
NELSON
www.tommynelson.com

A Division of Thomas Nelson, Inc.
www.ThomasNelson.com

Published in Nashville, Tennessee, by Tommy Nelson®, a
Division of Thomas Nelson, Inc. Visit us on the Web at
www.tommynelson.com

Unless otherwise indicated, Scripture quotations are from the
International Children's Bible®, *New Century Version*®, copyright
© 1986, 1988, 1999 by Tommy Nelson®, a Division of Thomas
Nelson, Inc.

Library of Congress Cataloging-in-Publication Data

Myers, Bill, 1953–
    My life as a walrus whoopee cushion / Bill Myers.
        p. cm. — (The incredible worlds of Wally McDoogle ; #16)
    Summary: When Wally, Opera, and Wall Street win the
Gazillion Dollar Lotto, they confront the dangers of greed and
materialism through a series of incidents involving bungling
bad guys, a break-in to the zoo, and a SWAT team.
    ISBN 0-8499-4025-7
    1. Lotteries Fiction. 2. Greed Fiction. 3. Zoos Fiction.
4. Christian life Fiction. 5. Humorous stories. I. Title.
II. Series: Myers, Bill, 1953–   . Incredible worlds of Wally
McDoogle ; #16.
PZ7.M98234My 1999
Fic—dc21   99-13459
                                                               CIP

Printed in the United States of America

01 02 03 04 05 PHX 13 12 11 10 9

To Jeff—
Thanks for the cool idea!

And to Mackenzie—
Thanks for the cool title!

"For the love of money is a root of all kinds of evil. Some people, eager for money, have wandered from the faith and pierced themselves with many griefs."

—1 Timothy 6:10 (NIV)

Contents

Chapter 1

Just for Starters . . .

The next time I get carried away with making a ton of money, just tie my shoelaces to a runaway freight train or shake my head to see if there's any part of my pea brain left rattling inside. Because . . . if I can't remember what I learned on this little McDoogle mishap, then my mind is majorly missing.

It all started when the state lotto got up to 2.1 gazillion dollars. Suddenly, everyone in town went crazy buying lotto tickets. Dads filled their briefcases, Moms filled their purses, and those who could only buy a few tickets at a time came back almost as often as my big brother did trying to pass his driver's test.

The point is, everybody had Lotto Fever in a big *I-don't-care-how-many-meals-we're-gonna-miss-I'm-buying-another-fifty-tickets!* kind of way.

Even us kids.

1

"Hey, Wally, *(munch-munch)* where you guys headed?" It was Opera, my best friend, the 'eating machine'. School had just let out, and he was catching up to Wall Street, my other best friend (even though she is a girl), and me.

"Off to buy lotto tickets!" I shouted. You always have to shout to Opera. The only thing he loves more than eating potato chips is listening to classical music—which explains the Walkman headphones surgically attached to his ears. "You want to go in as partners with us?" I asked.

"Nah, *(crunch-crunch)* nobody ever wins those things."

"We will," Wall Street shouted. She gave me a sly wink. "I've got a couple of systems all worked out to choose the winning number."

"No *(crunch-munch)* kidding?"

"You bet," Wall Street said. It was an obvious con job. Wall Street planned to make her first million by the time she was fourteen—most of it off of Opera and me.

She whipped out her calculator and punched a bunch of keys. "You see, you take the hypotenuse of a right triangle, multiply it by the latest Dow Jones Industrial Average, divide it by $E=MC^2$, and BINGO! You get the winning number!" (Wall Street could convince people of just about anything.)

"Really?" Opera cried.

"Oh, yeah!" Wall Street said. Then lowering her voice, she pretended to have even more inside information. "And, if that doesn't work," she glanced around, "there's always my super, top-secret tried-and-true method."

"What's *(munch-crunch)* that?" Opera whispered back.

"Eeny, meeny, miney, mo."

"Hey, I've heard of that one!" he cried.

"Rats, my secret's out. Oh, well," she shrugged. "I guess it's hard to keep anything a secret that works so perfectly."

That's all Opera needed to hear. Before you could say, "There's a fool born every minute," he dug into his pocket and pulled out a wad of bills. "Here, let me go in with you guys and buy some of those tickets."

Good ol' Opera—heart as big as a forest, mind as dumb as a stump.

"Hey, McDorkle!"

I looked up just in time to see Gary the Gorilla reaching for my throat. Fortunately, I took a breath just before he cut off my air supply. (Sometimes Gary forgets his own strength, which is easy to do when you're the only seventh grader who has to shave twice a day.)

"You guys buyin' lotto tickets?" he asked as he

lifted me off the ground and held me up face-to-face with him.

I wanted to answer, but it's hard to say anything when you're busy choking to death. I opened my mouth, but what came out was the usual: *Choke . . . Gasp . . . Cough . . . Wheeze . . .*

"Well, are you?" he demanded.

I gave an encore performance of my dying routine: *Wheeze . . . Cough . . . Gasp . . . Choke . . .*

"What's the matter, cat got your tongue?" he asked.

"Actually," Wall Street pointed out, "it's the bully that's got his throat."

"Oh." Realizing he might be the cause of my early death, he let go of my neck. I sort of slid down to the sidewalk . . . not dead but giving it some serious thought.

"I'm fillin' out my lotto numbers," I heard him say. "And I can't figure out what to put down for the last number—a five or a two."

"That's easy!" Opera said. "Wall Street here *(munch-crunch, crunch-munch)* has a system and—"

"Shh." Wall Street pretended to frown. "Don't give away all my secrets."

"Oh, *(crunch-munch)* never mind."

But it was too late. Opera had let the make-believe cat out of the make-believe bag. With one swift move, Gary reached down to Wall Street and lifted her up.

"You gots a secret for finding the winning number?" he growled into her face.

"No, . . ." she gasped, "I was just . . . making that . . . up."

"Oh." He must have believed her because he set her back down a lot gentler than he did me—a definite advantage of being a girl. Then he glared back at me—a definite disadvantage of me being me. "I need some help here, McDorkoid," he demanded.

Never wanting to disappoint Gary, let alone almost die twice in the same afternoon, I staggered to my feet. "If you only have two choices," I said, trying to rub his ring-around-the-collar fingerprints off my neck, "why don't you just flip for it. Heads, it'll be five—tails, it'll be two."

"Hey, that's a great idea!" He beamed.

I turned to Opera and Wall Street, pleased that I'd found a nonlethal solution until I noticed my feet were off the ground. Once again I was enjoying the wonderful aroma of Gary the Gorilla's breath.

"I'll just flip for a number," he said. "You come up heads, then I'll write down five. You come up tails, then I'll write down two."

Before I could point out that using coins might

be better than using me, he grabbed me by the chest and with one mighty heave sent me flying high into the air.

And with one mighty breath, I screamed my lungs out:

"AUGHhhh . . ."

Now, I really don't want to complain. I mean it's not Gary's fault he doesn't know his own strength . . . and I'm sure not every passenger in that 757 had a heart attack when they saw me shooting past their windows. Still, when I hit the ground, I did have one complaint.

"OAFF!"

It hurt.

And to make matters worse, instead of landing on my front or my back, I landed on my side. After I pried myself out of the asphalt and opened my eyes, I saw Gary looking down at me a little confused.

"Hey, you landed on your edge."

"I'm sorry," I groaned.

"That's okay." He suddenly broke into a grin and reached down to help me up.

I was grateful there were no hard feelings.

I was not grateful when he said, "Guess we gotta go best two out of three."

Suddenly he grabbed me, suddenly, I was flying through the air again, and suddenly, I was repeating my favorite phrase:

"AUGHhhh . . ."

* * * * *

There was no problem guessing which Lotto Mart was selling the lotto tickets. Something about a line of people stretching from here to infinity gave it away. But I was surprised by the number of poor people I saw standing in line.

"Some of these people can't afford to buy tickets," I whispered to Wall Street. "What are they doing here?"

"I guess they figure it's their only chance to stop being poor," she said.

"But the odds of winning are so small! Isn't that kind of taking advantage of them?" I asked.

She shrugged. "Sure, I guess."

"Is that fair?"

"What do you care?" she scoffed. "Just think of all their money that you'll be winning."

I didn't find a lot of comfort in her words. I found even less comfort in the next ones.

"Excuse me, ain't you Wally McDoogle?"

I turned to see a big man who'd just come out of the Lotto Mart. He had a dozen lotto tickets in his hands and wore a sweater with the words, "Save the Snails" printed on it.

If I'd sucked my breath in any harder, I would have sprained my lungs. He was one of the terrorists I'd put in jail way back in *My Life As Dinosaur Dental Floss.*

He looked at me, waiting for an answer.

I knew it was time to act. I knew it was time to do what I'm a pro at. I knew it was time to make up as many excuses as I could think of!

"It wasn't my fault," I blurted out. "I'm not the one who thought the rhubarb sauce was nuclear fuel! And, you really can't blame me for getting the fire hose caught in the Tyrannosaurus Rex's teeth, besides how'd I know the President would—"

"Easy, pal, easy." He chuckled. "You wasn't responsible."

"I wasn't?" (This was obviously a first.) "Are you sure?"

He nodded. "Actually, I'm grateful for dat time in prison. It like, showed me the errors of my way. The fact is, if it weren't for you, I'd a never learnt that crime don't pay."

"So, you're not mad at me?" I asked.

"Of course not." He smiled a semi-toothless

smile. "Oh, speakin' of crime, don't you know that
kids under eighteen can't buy lotto tickets?"

"We can't?" Wall Street sounded surprised.

"That's right."

"But we've got all this . . . *burp* . . . money."
Opera had finished his chips and was now working on his soda.

For a moment, the Big Lug couldn't answer. All
he could do was stare at the wad of money in
Opera's hands.

"What are we going to . . . *belch* . . . do with all
this cash?" Opera asked.

Finally, Big Lug found his voice. "Tells ya what
I'm gonna do." He reached for one of his tickets
and handed it to Opera. "I'll sell ya one of mine."

"No . . . *BELCH* . . . kidding . . . *BURRRP?*"
(That was a good one.)

"Absolutely!" Big Lug grinned. "One for the price
of four."

Before I could stop him, Opera handed over
all his money. "It's a deal!" (The only thing
worse than Opera's eating habits were his busi-
ness skills.)

I spun around to Wall Street, hoping she would
say something. But she was too overcome with
grief to speak. (The poor girl's heart was shattered
that someone else had beaten her to all of Opera's
money.)

"Here you go," Big Lug said. (Obviously, he had no sympathy for the intellectually challenged.) "Number 333777," he read the ticket's number as he handed it to Opera. "Sounds pretty lucky to me."

"Thanks, Mister! . . . *BURP*."

"Hey, wait a minute," Wall Street said.

But Big Lug wasn't sticking around. "Sorry, gotta go."

Before either of us could protest, he had stuffed Opera's money into his pocket and started down the street. "Good luck on tomorrow's drawing," he yelled, then let out a good laugh.

"Yeah, right," Wall Street muttered.

"Tell me about it," I grumbled.

"Thanks a lot!" Opera shouted back. And then turning to us, he grinned. "Boy, aren't we lucky."

Wall Street and I could only roll our eyes. Little did we realize how *un*lucky we were all about to become.

Chapter 2

A Little Snack

Dinner was a delicious combination of fried celery, boiled bread, and cremated hot dogs. (If you guessed it was my little sister Carrie's night to cook, you guessed right. If you guessed she told Mom she wanted to do it all on her own, you guessed right again.)

I managed to survive the so-called cooking by secretly stuffing the remains of my death-on-a-plate into my pockets. (I used to slip them to our pet cat, but Dad was getting tired of rushing Collision, our kitty, to the vet every time Carrie cooked.)

Anyway, after living through another meal, I decided to unwind by writing a little superhero story. That's what I want to do if I survive the seventh grade—I want to be a writer.

Of course, that makes Dad a bit nervous. He wants me to follow in his footsteps and be a real man . . . just like my older twin brothers, Burt and

Brock. Unfortunately, being a real man also involves trying out for every sport ever invented. No problem, except I'm such a lightweight I couldn't even make the badminton team— although once they did ask if they could use me as the badminton birdie.

Anyway, after putting aside my homework, I reached for Ol' Betsy, my laptop computer, and started to write.

"B.B. Boy?" our superhero's mom calls from the hallway outside his bedroom. "Wake-up, Dear. It's time to rise and shine."

Our incredibly good-looking and majorly muscular superhero stretches his incredible good-looking and majorly muscular superhero body.

"Oh, Mom," he groans. "Do I have to?"

"I'm afraid so, Dear. It's time to put that incredibly good-looking and majorly muscular superhero body to work."

"But Mom!"

"Don't 'But Mom' me. It's another beautiful day for halting hateful hooligans, beating bad-boy bullies, and stopping sinisterly sneaky spies. Besides

there's an important e-mail from
President Clington waiting for you."

"Another one?" our hero moans. "Don't
tell me he wants me to save the world
again? Didn't I do that yesterday?"

"No, Dear. Yesterday you saved the uni-
verse. Last week, you saved the world.
Besides, this message is labeled,
URGENT."

"That's how he always labels them,"
complains our incredibly good-looking
and majorly muscular superhero. (Guess
I've beaten that phrase to death,
haven't I?) He throws off the aluminum
blankets, slips on his steel-plated
jeans, and clanks across the metal
floor. (And you were afraid that this
story was getting too normal, weren't
you?)

He reaches for the ten-inch-thick
steel door and opens it:

CREAK.

Out in the hall he spots his mom holding a neatly pressed shirt and wearing
her gas mask.

"Here you go, Dear," she says as she

hands him the shirt. "I've only sprayed
on three coats of bulletproof plastic,
so please do your best not to breathe on
it."

"Thanks, Mom," he says as he takes the
shirt. Unfortunately, he accidentally
breathes on the picture that's hanging
in the hall, and it immediately bursts
into flames.

"Oh, Dear!" his mother cries through
her gas mask as she quickly whips out
a fire extinguisher and puts out the
flames. "You've really got to be more
careful about that breath of yours."

"Sorry," B.B. Boy says as he sadly
shuts the door. Poor guy. It's not like
he has the worst breath in the world.
Actually it's the worst in the galaxy.

No one's sure what made B.B. (alias
Bad Breath) Boy's breath so bad. Some
say it came from his mom eating too many
onions the nine months before he was
born. Others insist it came from his
dad, a health food nut, making him swal-
low all those garlic pills. (It may not
have given him permanent bad breath, but
it sure cut down on vampire attacks.)
Whatever the case, Bad Breath Boy's

breath is bad enough to stop a mule...
usually by killing it.

That's why the government always calls
him when they're in trouble. And that's
why the President is calling him now.
Quicker than you can say, "This guy's
even stranger than Floss Man, Tidy Guy,
or any of those other superheroes of
mine," B.B. Boy grabs a bottle of
Listerine, gives a quick gargle, and
heads for his computer.

The effects of the mouthwash will only
last a few seconds, but that's all he'll
need to quickly read the screen and turn
away before his breath melts it.

He snaps on the computer and punches
up the e-mail. There's the message:

B.B. Boy:¶
The dastardly disastrous Dollar Dude is on
the loose . . .¶

(Insert scary music here.)¶

He's escaped from the prison of the
incurably rich and has launched a satellite.
It captures all the sunbeams and changes
them into Megabuck Beams . . . special

beams that transform everything they
touch into money.¶

**"Everything?" our hero asks under
his breath.**

Everything . . . trees, buildings, little
children.¶

**Our hero looks up from the screen
and for one brief second wonders if he
can talk his little sister into going
outside and getting a tan. Then, realizing he's the superhero of this story,
and superheroes are supposed to be role
models for impressionable readers like
yourselves, he turns back to the moni-
tor and continues to read:**

We've already fired missiles at it, but its
rays turn the rockets into twenty-dollar
bills that flutter back to earth. You're our
only hope. Perhaps your breath can
dissolve the satellite before it's too late.
Good luck. God bless. Get going!¶

**Without wasting another moment, our
hero spins away from the computer screen**

to look out the window. Unfortunately, the mouthwash has worn off and his breath melts the glass, but not before he sees the leaves on the trees outside turning into five-dollar bills and dropping to the ground. Then there are the shingles on the roof across the street that are turning into twenties and blowing away. Finally, there are the clothes on his next-door neighbor, Mrs. Hubba-Hubba, which are all...well, let's just say it's a good thing the window is melting and getting all cloudy so he can no longer see out.

Something has to be done. Who knows what dastardly deeds Dollar Dude is deciding to do? Who knows what absolute awfulness this astonishing author will author? Who knows—

"Wally, it's time for bed."

I glanced up from Ol' Besty. "Okay, Mom," I shouted. "Just give me a second."

I looked back at the story. It was definitely one of my strangest beginnings. I mean, on the McDoogle Weirdness Scale of one to ten, it was definitely pushing an eleven. I figured lots of the strangeness had to do with me thinking about all that money Wall Street, Opera, and I hoped to win in tomorrow's lotto. Little did I realize that the strangeness I'd been writing would be nothing compared to the strangeness I'd soon be living!

* * * * *

"The walrus, whose scientific name is *Odobenus rosmarus*, resides in *blah-blah-blah-blah* and primarily eats *yadda-yadda-yadda-yadda . . .*"

It was another boring field trip brought to us courtesy of Mr. Reptenson, our boring science teacher. This time our class was at the zoo. We'd all gathered around the walrus area at the top of a hill as he (Mr. Reptenson, not the walrus) continued his lecture:

"The male can grow up to twelve feet long and can weigh three thousand pounds . . ."

Don't get me wrong, I like getting out of school (and pretending we're learning something) as much as the next guy. But Reptile Man (that's what we call him for short) can take the world's most exciting subject and turn it into a world-class yawning event.

"However and furthermore . . ." he continued, "in which case, one can only speculate . . ."

Seriously, if you ever get the choice between listening to one of his lectures or hearing the "I Love You, You Love Me" theme song a million times (as if we haven't already), trust me, go for the purple dinosaur.

But that wasn't much of a problem for Wall Street, Opera, and me. Today, we had a lot more important things on our minds. That's why we hung out toward the back of the group whispering to one another. At the moment we were behind the popcorn wagon arguing over the only subject we'd talked about since we bought our lotto ticket . . .

"And I'm telling you," Wall Street said, "as the brains of the group, I should get half the money. You and Opera should split what's left over."

Opera tried to answer, "But—"

I cut him off. "Listen, if it weren't for me, that guy would never have sold Opera the ticket in the first place."

"But—"

"And what a great deal your friend gave us, too," she argued.

"But—"

"Hey, it wasn't my fault," I whispered.

"But—"

"That ticket is rightfully mine!" she said.

"But—"

"No way, it's really mine!"

"But—"

Finally, we both turned to Opera and demanded, "What?"

"Actually . . . ," he pulled the ticket from his pocket and grinned, ". . . it's mine."

"What are you doing carrying that around?" Wall Street cried. "It could get lost!"

"I've got it safe in my pocket."

"That's not good enough," she said as she reached for it. "You better give that to me so it won't get—"

Unfortunately, Opera quickly pulled it away.

Unfortunatelier (don't try using this word in school, kids), he pulled it in my direction, which meant I lunged for it, instead.

Unfortunateliest, I grabbed it, but bumped into the popcorn wagon pretty hard . . . which released the brake, which sent it rolling down the hill.

No problem, except for the part where I was standing directly in front of it.

Well, I had been standing directly in front of it. Now I was—

K-BAMB!

"AUGHhhh . . ."

riding on the front of it!

Since the hill was steep, in a major Mount Everest kind of way, the wagon took off like a shot.

"Wally, come back here!" Wall Street shouted.

"I want my ticket!" Opera cried.

"You'd better pay attention because we're having a quiz!" Reptile Man yelled.

I would have loved to answer any of those requests, but it's hard on answer when you've become the hood ornament on a popcorn wagon. Especially, when it looks like that popcorn wagon is about to set the world's land speed record!

"Look out!" I cried to a little kid who leaped to the side just in time.

"Coming through!" I shouted to a mother who just managed to shove her baby carriage out of the way.

"Somebody move that cotton candy cart, before we—"

K-SMASH!

Well, two out of three wasn't bad.

So, there I was rolling down the hill, squished between a cotton candy cart in front of me and a popcorn wagon in the back. Talk about *meals on wheels*. I must have looked like the world's weirdest sandwich. And with all that junk food on both sides, it was probably good that there was a little meat in the middle . . . unfortunately, that "little meat" was me!

The good news was that wherever we went I wouldn't starve. The bad news was that the hill had leveled off. Normally, that would have been good news, too, except for the

TOOT! TOOT!

. . . miniature train ride . . .

CLANG! CLANG!

that was heading straight toward me!

TOOT! TOOT!
CLANG! CLANG!

Once again, it was time for clear thinking. Once again, it was time to do what I did best. Once again, I opened my mouth and screamed my lungs out:

"AUGHHHHH!"

Chapter 3

Zoo Goo

So, there I was racing toward the little engine that *could* (could kill me, that is), preparing for my daily recommended dosage of pain, when I noticed an important fact: I could actually steer my little concession stand. That's right! By leaning to the left, I could veer to the left. By leaning to the right, I could veer to the right.

Great news. Now, all I had to do was see where I was veering! (Not an easy task when your glasses are coated in two inches of cotton candy, better make that three inches . . . er, four.) The point is that the cotton candy machine was going to beat the band and all that pink, hairy stuff was blowing back into my face. (Better make that five inches.) Cool, if you're a cotton candy nut. Not so cool if you're trying to veer for your life.

TOOT! TOOT!

CLANG! CLANG!

But beggars can't be choosers! I had to make a choice. If I was lucky, I'd steer the right way and miss the train all together. If I was unlucky, well, this could be the shortest Wally McDoogle book in history.

After a short prayer, where I carefully reminded God of all the good stuff I'd ever done (which explains why it was so short), I decided I should lean to the right.

But, knowing how bad my luck was, I decided to lean to the left because I actually wanted to lean to the right. Make sense? But knowing my luck was worse than normal bad luck, I decided to lean to the right—because I thought I should lean to the left because I had really wanted to lean to the right. Then again, if that's what I was thinking, maybe I should—

KER-SPLAT

Well, that took care of my thinking, and my believing in luck. (It nearly took care of my breathing, too.) After wasting all that time trying to decide, I'd run smack-dab into the middle of my little Thomas the Train buddy.

TOOT! TOOT!
CLANG! CLANG!

(Okay, knock it off, will you!)

By now the cotton candy cart, popcorn wagon, and myself were so tangled together, it was hard to tell where one left off and the other began— though I did notice the cart and wagon seemed to be bleeding a lot less than me. I also noticed I was starting to slip. I hung on and turned my head to look through the window of the popcorn wagon. All in all it wasn't a bad view; it would have been a terrific way to see the rest of the zoo, except I really couldn't see. Instead of cotton candy all over the place, I was now peering through a window of popping corn.

(Aren't you getting hungry reading this? Sorry I couldn't have hit a lemonade stand to wash it all down.)

I peered through all those bouncy little kernels of buttery delight, until I caught a glimpse of an approaching train trestle. An approaching train trestle could only mean there was an approaching drop-off . . . no doubt, the hundred-foot if-you-fall-this-could-sure-ruin-your-day kind of drop-off.

Now I had two more choices to make. Wait and hope I could get all the way across the trestle

without sliding off and falling to my death, or jump
now and get killed just a little bit sooner.

Decisions, decisions.

But being the type who likes to put off until
tomorrow what I could do today (especially when
it involves dying), I decided to hang on.

The good news was that we made it about
halfway across the gorge before I really started
slipping. The bad news was, *half*way is not the
same as *all* the way.

Suddenly, the cart, the wagon, and yours truly
slid from the train and began to fall. To be honest, I wasn't too worried about the falling—it was
hitting the ground that had me concerned.

Fortunately, we didn't get to that part just
yet. We had to make a few stops along on the way.
First, there was the obligatory landing in the top
of a pine tree,

SNAP, CRACKLE, . . . BOING!

which bounced us back into the air until we
came down and

K-BAMB!

landed on the pitched roof of some building.
But, since my cart and wagon buddies still had

their wheels, our little McDoogle Mishap wasn't
entirely over. (Oh, no! That would be too easy.)
 With all the wheels still working, we started

roll . . . roll . . . roll . . . rolling down the roof
until

"AUGH!"
K-RASH

we hit the ground. But the fun and games
weren't over yet. We just kept on rolling . . .
down another hill . . . and straight toward
Monkey Land.
 The good news was that we managed to

K-BASH!

run into a lemonade stand just for you. (See
how thoughtful I am.) The bad news was that

K-RANG!

I discovered that steel bars to monkey cages
hurt worse than food carts, trains, treetops, and
roofs combined.
 I don't know how long I lay there unconscious,
but when I finally woke up I was sure I'd died and

gone to heaven. But then I finally opened my eyes
and saw the scariest angel ever. Granted, my
glasses were still pretty smeared with cotton
candy, but the big nostrils and huge furry face
staring down at me were terrifying.

"AUGH!"

I didn't mean to scream, but it's hard not to when
you're scared half to death. (Well, actually, in my
case, I figured I was scared *completely* to death.)

But instead of offering words of comfort, the
angel leaped back and let go an unearthly . . .

SHRIEK!

To which I calmly replied:

"AUGH! AUGH!"

To which the angel replied:

SHRIEK! SHRIEK!

To which I . . . well, you get the picture. It was
only then that I looked down and saw the angel
had a tail. And it was only then that I realized I
wasn't in heaven, but the *other* place!

Fortunately, it didn't look like the creature was in the mood to torment me with any pitch-forks. Instead, he reached down and raised a handful of popcorn to his mouth. Sadly, I real-ized my pal, the popcorn wagon, hadn't made it to the good place either. (By the way, where do concession stands go when they die? Not that anyone really cares . . . unless, of course, it's Opera.)

Anyway, the hideous creature took a sniff of the popcorn, then a nibble, then threw it away in dis-gust. With the other hand, he raised a banana to his mouth and began to eat. *Oh, no,* I thought, *even when you're dead they make you eat your fruits and vegetables!*

Then, with great effort, I raised up on one elbow and looked around.

It was worse than I expected! I wasn't in the other place at all! Somehow, someway, I'd been thrown through the bars and had landed smack-dab in the middle of Monkey Land!

No problem, except for the dozens of wild apes and monkeys that were slowly closing in—dozens of furry faces, little eyes, and not so little fangs. It was about then that I recalled how great passing out had been. So, looking for something to do to kill the time before they killed me, I decided to give it another try. . . .

* * * * *

"You say this sort of thing happens all the time?" the head zookeeper asked Dad.

"Well, not all the time," Dad answered. "Sometimes when he sleeps, nothing much happens. But when he's awake . . . well, let's just say that Wallace is the only living human who has been declared a National Disaster Area."

"Amazing."

"That's one word for it," Dad said.

All three of us . . . Dad, me, and Mr. Zookeeper, sat in the main office of the zoo discussing the problem. Well, they did the discussing. I just sort of sat there doing a lot of praying. I was glad they'd rescued me from the cage. I was not glad about what might happen next.

"You know, we really should press charges," Mr. Zookeeper was saying.

"I understand," Dad agreed.

"But," Mr. Zookeeper sighed, "since it wasn't intentional, I guess we won't. Although," he turned to me, "we will expect full reimbursement for the damaged items."

I nodded so hard my head almost broke.

Suddenly, the intercom buzzed.

"Excuse me." Mr. Zookeeper reached over and pressed a button. "Yes."

"Mr. Chambers, this is Lawrence at the leopard's cage. It's feeding time, and I'm having trouble with one of the locks. Could you hit the override for me?"

"Certainly." With that the man rose and crossed over to some fancy computer. He pulled a notebook from the shelf above it, read something inside, and then entered a few numbers on the keyboard. There was a brief *hum* and a *click* over the intercom and then Lawrence's voice answered: "Thank you, sir."

"No problem," Mr. Zookeeper answered. "We'll have the electrician check out the problem in the morning."

With that he turned back to Dad. "Where was I? Oh, yes. There will be a sizable cost in replacing all of the equipment your son has destroyed. And, of course, . . ." Mr. Zookeeper rambled on for a few more minutes about the cost and everything until it was finally Dad's turn.

Dad's speech was the one he used after all my little mishaps. The one where he talks about the special bank account he's set up to pay for my catastrophes as well as the various insurance polices he's taken out on me. It was all pretty normal.

Unfortunately, none of us realized it then, but what had happened at the zoo that afternoon was small potatoes compared to what would be happening there that night.

Chapter 4

And the Winning Number Is . . .

The lotto drawing wasn't until 9:30 that night, which meant I had plenty of time to battle my homework and get ready for bed. My latest enemy was complex fractions, complete with all those wonderful little things called *numerators* and *denominators*. (I say, just bring in the Terminator and divide and conquer.)

The good news was that by 9:00 I was done. The bad news was that I still had a half-hour to kill before the drawing. To say I was excited about the lotto was an understatement. It was like my birthday, Christmas, and a day without being beaten up after school all wrapped into one. And with a lucky number like 333777, how could we miss?

Of course, I could have used that extra time to think about all the trouble my stroll through Greed Land had caused at the zoo, and how all that arguing over the ticket had ended up causing

so much destruction to property and to me. But
it's kinda hard to think about the dangers of wanting money, when all you can do is think about getting that money. So, instead of dwelling on the
errors of my ways, I whipped out Ol' Betsy and
went back to my story. Yes, sir, nothing makes time
fly (and helps you avoid reality) like a little superhero writing.

When we last left B.B. Boy, everything
was turning into dollar bills, thanks
to the lowdown doings of that dastardly,
dynamic, and dangerously destruc-
tive...(I think that about wraps it up
for Ds, don't you?) Dollar Dude.

Quicker than you can say, "Wait a
minute" (I still don't get how a person
can be a superhero just because he has
bad breath), B.B. Boy throws on his
breathproof coat and races for the door.

Outside, it's worse than he fears.
Buildings are collapsing into mounds of
twenty-dollar bills; light poles are dis-
solving into tens and fluttering away;
and those strange-looking VW Beetles are
turning into piles of fives. (Well, I
guess every cloud has a silver lining.)

Quickly, he slips on his pair of
Nifty-Spiffy Detecto Goggles (just
$19.95 at superhero stores everywhere)
and looks up into the sky. He lets out
a gasp, which downs a flock of pigeons
flying overhead. But the falling fowls
offer few frustrations for our fearless
fellow (and you thought the Ds were
bad). Because overhead he has spotted...

(Insert more bad guy music.)

Dollar Dude's satellite as it's changing the sunlight into ugly Megabuck
beams!

B.B. Boy lets out another gasp (which
takes care of that family of squirrels
in the nearby tree).

He spins around to the townspeople,
but nobody seems to care. They're all
just grabbing as much money as possi-
ble. Everywhere, people are fighting and
pushing and hollering. "People! People!"
our hero shouts while leaping atop a
stack of bills so he can be heard.

"Augh...augh!" the people shout, while
racing away from B.B. Boy's breath so
they can breathe.

But he continues, "Can't you see that this is the work of that not so nice and neurotically nutsoid...

(Try to insert more bad guy music, even though all of the musician's instruments have turned into bills.)

Dollar Dude! If we don't stop him now, the entire world will turn into money!"

"All right!" the people shout.

"No, it's not all right!" our hero cries. "If everything turns into money, what will you eat, what will you wear, where will you live?"

But no one listens. All anyone cares about is grabbing cash.

B.B. Boy has reasoned with them all he can. Now it's time to do what he can do, which is why he decides to do what he does (or something like that). In one swift move, he leaps onto the back of a passing skateboard.

The skateboarder looks over his shoulder and cries, "'Sup, dude?"

B.B. Boy starts to answer, which unfortunately means having to breathe. As soon as his breath hits the skateboarder, the kid breaks into a coughing fit. The boy pushes harder and faster, hoping to somehow get away from our hero. Of course, he could have just leaped off the board, but that would require thinking, and B.B. Boy's breath was already clouding his mind. (The fact that he's a skateboarder probably means he has his mind in the clouds, anyway.)

Harder and harder the groggy, gagging guy pushes. Faster and faster the groggy, gagging guy goes. (Hey, those were easy, just wait a couple of paragraphs.)

But going fast is not the same as going up. And *up* happens to be the direction of the satellite.

Suddenly, as luck would have it, a giant eagle swoops down. Realizing he better make his move before you (the reader) complain about all of these coincidences, our hero leaps from the back of the skateboard and onto the back of the bird.

But Ol' Birdbrain isn't crazy about the idea and, he, too, tries to get away. In desperation...(okay, here we go now; be

careful not to sprain your tongue)...in
desperation, the fantastically fine
feathered fowl ferociously flaps his fab-
ulously feathered flappers furiously.
(Say that with a mouthful of birdseed!)
Soon they are so high above the earth
that there is not much air to breathe.
This is fine with the eagle, since not
much air means not much bad breath—
but it isn't great with B.B. Boy, since
not much breath means not much life.

Refusing to be distracted by such
minor inconveniences, our hero reaches
into his pocket and pulls out his
Neato-Keen Oxygen Mask. (Sold at those
same superhero stores, but with a $5.00
rebate. So, get them while supplies
last.) He slips it over his face and
looks up.

What luck! Just a few more miles overhead is the satellite.

Thanking his bird buddy for the lift,
our hero leaps high into the air!
However, since his only superhero power
is bad breath (and nothing neat like
being able to fly around or owning a
cool bat cape or anything), he just

<pre>
       drops...
        like...
         a...
          r
            o
              c
                k
                 ✹
</pre>

But, as even more luck would have it, the Space Shuttle just happens to be passing by. (Hey, it's my superhero story. If you can do better, go ahead and write your own...but, uh, er, please make sure my name's on it when you send it to the bookstores, just in case it's a hit. Thanks.)

With another leap, our hero grabs onto the wing of the shuttle. (Fortunately, its heat tiles prevent his breath from doing too much structural damage.) In just a matter of seconds, they have reached the height of the satellite. With fond farewells and promises to write, B.B. Boy lets go of the shuttle and floats toward Dollar Dude's dangerously dubious doohickey. That's when he hears the chilling words:

"Thanks for falling into my little
trap, B.B. Brat."

Suddenly, our hero spots a pair of eyes
peering over the top of the satellite...a
pair of eyes connected to a face connected
to a body connected to a pair of arms that
are turning the satellite around until
its beam points directly at B.B. Boy!

Great gobs of greenbacks! What will
protect our hero from becoming a bunch
of bucks? A heap of hundreds? A ton of
twenties? (And, more important, if you
send that superhero story to the bookstores, remember to spell my name right.
It's M-c-D-o-o—)

"Wally!" my little sister, Carrie, shouted. "Come
on down, the drawing's about to begin."

"Be right there," I shouted back.

I quickly saved the story and shut Ol' Betsy
down. Don't get me wrong, writing the Bad Breath
Boy adventure was fine, but it's nothing compared
to living my own. Unfortunately, if I had known
what awaited me, I would have stayed up there
writing for the rest of my life. Because writing a
crazed, whacked-out adventure is a lot easier than
living one.

* * * * *

I raced down the stairs as fast as I could.
Well, actually, a little faster than I could ... which
meant I did the usual stumbling, falling, and
bouncing down the steps. No biggie. Everyone in
my family was used to it, which explains the extra
padding Dad had installed at the bottom. That
way when I landed ...

K-WOOSH ...

I seldom broke any of the real important body
parts.

Everybody was down in the family room doing
what they did best:

— Dad was looking over the bills and grum-
   bling, "Who keeps turning the thermostat
   above 60?"
— Burt and Brock, my superjock brothers, were
   putting down another half-gallon of ice
   cream apiece and working on their multipli-
   cation tables (which is a little embarrassing
   for eleventh graders, but I did mention they
   were football players, right?).
— Carrie was flipping through a cookbook,
   preparing for next week's dinner.

— Collision, our cat, was cowering in the corner in fear of next week's dinner.

— And Mom, who looked up from folding laundry, was asking me, "Oh, Wally, are you sure you don't want to wear these *Star Wars* undershorts another year?"

Snickers filled the room.

"Mom!"

"But you look so cute parading around in your little Obi-Wan Kenobis."

"MOM!"

"Oh, all right."

"Shh, it's on," my older brother Burt said. (Or was it Brock? I can't always keep them straight.)

I joined him in front of the TV as Dad cranked up the volume. (He may have been busy doing bills, but he was still King of the Remote.)

"You really don't think you're gonna win," asked Brock, my other brother (or was it Burt?).

"Hey, he's got just as much chance of winning as the next person," Carrie said.

"Thank you," I smiled.

"I mean, it's not like he has to be smart or anything."

My smile kinda wavered.

"Yeah," Burt agreed, "or good-looking, or talented—"

"Or anything at all," Brock jumped in.

"Exactly!" Carrie nodded, pleased that they now saw her point. (Ah, little sisters, so young, so innocent . . . so clueless.)

"Shh," Burt said, "the first number's comin' up."

Instead of people drawing tickets out of a box, they had a little machine that spit out numbered Ping-Ponglike balls. I watched in breathless anticipation as the first white ball rolled into place. It had the number 3 written on it!

"All right!" I shouted, practically jumping out of my skin. "That's my first number!"

"Just luck," Burt scoffed. "Never happen again. What's the rest of your number?"

"It's 333777," I said. I glanced over at Mom and saw she wasn't even paying attention. She just kept on folding the laundry. "Mom," I cried, "don't you care? I'm on my way to becoming a gazillionaire!"

"I hope not," was all she said.

The second number came up: 3 again!

"Way to go, Wally!" Carrie cried.

I grinned and threw another look toward Mom. "What do you mean, *you hope not*?" I asked.

She glanced up. "I hope you don't win."

"What's that supposed to mean?"

"It means I've seen too many lives ruined over greed, money, and gambling."

The third number came up: another 3!

I couldn't believe it! I was halfway there! It was like a dream! Mom could talk all she wanted, but money was money! And, if I actually won, who knew what cool and incredible things could happen.

"Wally," my dad asked absently, "where'd you get that ticket?"

"Well, um," I stammered. But before I could answer, the next number came up and . . .

It was a 7!

By now everyone in the room was watching. Mom included. Even Dad had managed to look up from scowling at the bills.

The next ball rolled into place . . . 7!

One more to go. By now we'd all quit breathing. Even Collision . . . though I suspect that might have had to do with Carrie giving him some of tonight's leftovers. (I guess that's enough cracks about her cooking isn't it?)

Anyway, the ball rolled into place and came up . . . 7!

I couldn't believe it. For a moment we all sat stunned as the winning number flashed on the screen:

333777

That was it! That was my number! I was a winner!

Suddenly, the room exploded. Everyone was jumping up and down . . . even Mom and Dad.

"2.1 gazillion dollars!" I shouted. "2.1 gazillion dollars! 2.1 gazillion dollars!"

"You're superrich!" Carrie cried. "You're superrich! You're superrich!"

"You're my favorite brother!" Burt and Brock yelled. "You're my favorite brother! You're my favorite brother!"

It was great—everyone shouting, slapping me on the back, pretending to actually like me. In fact, we were having so much fun I barely heard the phone. When I finally realized it was ringing, I raced to it and picked it up. "Hello?" I yelled.

"We won!" Wall Street shouted on the other end. "We won! We won! We won!"

"I know!" I shouted. "I know! I know! I know!"

"Just hang on to that ticket!" she cried. "Don't let it out of your sight. I'll be right over."

"What ticket?" I shouted. "Opera has it. Let's meet at his house!"

"No, you have it."

"No, Opera has it."

"Wally, you grabbed it out of Opera's hand just before you crashed into the popcorn wagon and did your Master of Disaster thing."

"No way, I—" Suddenly, I went cold. She was right. I did grab it. And I hung on to it through the whole ordeal . . . the crashing of carts, the riding on trains, the bouncing off of pine trees. I even remember holding on to it as I crashed into the monkey cage . . . where I lost consciousness.

"Wally?" Wall Street yelled. "Talk to me! Wally? Tell me you have the ticket! *Wally?*"

I tried to answer, but it's hard to answer when you've forgotten to breathe.

"Wally! Where is it? *Where's the lotto ticket?*"

Finally something came out of my mouth. I can't be sure exactly what it was, but it sounded a little like: "The monkeys have it."

Chapter 5

The Plan Sickens . . .

For the most part, things were okay. Other than winning 2.1 gazillion dollars, losing it, and having to find it all over again, things were perfectly normal.

Wall Street, Opera, and I had agreed to meet down at the Grease O'Burger Cafe. Their motto:

> *If You Gotta Chew to Make It Slide Down, It Ain't Greasy Enough.*

It was just across the street from the zoo and would be a great place to decide what we would do next. There, over a steaming hot plate of salt-saturated grease (with a thread of potato slipped in so they could legally call them French fries), we could discuss our plan—a plan that involved:

1. Going back to the zoo.
2. Miraculously finding the lotto ticket.
3. Becoming filthy rich.

Now, I admit there were a few details to work out, especially with the second one, which is why we had to meet. But before the meeting, I had a couple of other problems to deal with first . . . like getting out of the house.

I didn't have to worry about Mom and Dad, they were too busy calling every relative, every friend, and every friend of every relative to tell them the good news. No, my problem was a bit more complicated than that . . . like getting dressed.

Ever try putting on your clothes when you're gonzo crazy about winning 2.1 gazillion dollars and losing it all in the same day? No? Then you really can't laugh when I tell you I accidentally put my pants on backward. (Hey, it can happen to anybody. Well, almost anybody.)

What could *not* happen to anybody was putting my pants on backward *and* my shirt on upside down. (I thought it buttoned kinda funny, but didn't notice anything until I tried to tuck it in and nearly suffocated myself.)

Not a pretty sight.

Then there were my brothers. On good days,

they just ignore me. On the not so good ones, they
turn me upside down and use my head as a toilet
brush. But not tonight. Tonight I was king of the
house. Of course, I didn't bother telling them that
I'd also lost the ticket (what they didn't know
wouldn't hurt me). The point is that as soon as I
stepped out of my room, they were all over me like
fleas on a dog, ketchup over fries, maple syrup
over fried pickles. (Okay sorry. I promised not to
pick on Carrie's cooking, didn't I?)

"Excuse me, Wally, could I pick up your room?"

"Excuse me, Wally, could I zip up your coat?"

"Excuse me, Wally, could I floss your teeth?"

See what I mean? Oh, I knew they just wanted
to be my buddy so they could get their greedy, not-
so-little-hands on all of my money. Well, it wouldn't
work. I was smarter than that. Besides it was my
money, not theirs. *Mine.* Mine, mine, mine. (Well,
it would be as soon as I found the ticket.) I
didn't know it then, but my greed was already getting majorly out of hand. (Unfortunately, it would
get a lot more major before it got minor.)

When I finally headed out the door and down
the sidewalk, I saw that my neighbors were no
different. Like my brothers, they were also trying
to butter me up. Everywhere I looked they were
smiling, grinning, or nodding at me. I figured
either my folks had called them up with the good

news or they just naturally sensed my sudden superiority.

Yes, sir, as far as I could tell, being rich really did make you a greater person. It wasn't until I glanced at my reflection in a window that I realized there might be another reason for all the attention . . . I was wearing my undershorts *over* my pants instead of *under*. (Hey, I told you I was nervous.)

Deciding this was no time to make a fashion statement, I dashed home and rearranged my wardrobe. After stopping by a mirror to make sure every arm, leg, and head was sticking out of the right opening, I headed back outside. I was grateful I'd made it through all those minitraumas. Now, I could focus on the maxitrauma coming up . . . the one where I'd have to face Opera and Wall Street.

* * * * *

I really didn't want to keep them waiting. I mean, right now I wasn't exactly high on their list of friends and the less I did to make them angry the better. Unfortunately, all the dressing delays did make me a little late. In fact, by the time I got there, Opera was already finishing off an order of fries. (Only a few remained floating in the inch-thick puddle of grease on his plate.)

"Glad you could make it," Wall Street said, scowling hard at me.

"Burp," Opera agreed.

"Sorry I'm late," I said, "I know you're a little upset right now. But you've got nothing to worry about. I've got it all figured out."

"Really?" Wall Street raised an eyebrow.

"Belch?" Opera asked.

I nodded. "We go across the street to the zoo, one of you crawls back into that monkey cage and—"

"One of *us*?" Wall Street interrupted.

"Well, yeah. I mean, it was scary enough for me to go in there the first time. You can't expect me to be the one to go in again."

They both stared at me.

"Come on," I insisted, "I went to all that effort of losing it, the least one of you could do is . . ."

Their look continued.

"All right . . . *I'll* crawl back into the cage, and *I'll* find the ticket."

"Sounds like a plan to me," Wall Street said.

"I'll wait here and have another order of fries," Opera agreed.

"Great," I sighed.

"But you know, we still have one little problem," Wall Street said.

"What's that?"

"The zoo's locked up."

"Mu metter mafe mat mwee mwitle mwoblems," Opera added. He'd fished out the last fry from the grease and was scarfing it down.

"What?" I asked.

He repeated himself. "You better make that three little problems."

"What are the other two?" I asked.

"Good evening, boys and girls," a male voice boomed from behind me.

"That's one," Opera said.

"I hoped I'd never see you brats again," another voice bellowed.

"That's the other."

I spun around to see my old buddy, Big Lug. With him was his woman partner from our Save the Snail days. But before any of us could get too sentimental about old times, she snapped, "You're sure these are the creeps who stole our lotto ticket?"

I don't want to be too critical, but it didn't look like prison life had done much to improve her manners, or Big Lug's diction.

"Dat's right," Big Lug said, "333777. Dat's the number dat won, and dat's the number they tooks from me."

"Hold it, wait a minute." Wall Street interrupted. "We bought that ticket from you fair and square."

"Is that true?" the woman asked Big Lug.

"I uh, well, dat is to say . . . listen," he complained,

"you can't expect me to remember all the details."

"Well, I remember," Wall Street said. "In fact, Opera here gave you four times what you paid for it. Isn't that right, Opera?"

"Burp." Opera nodded.

"That's right," I added. "You were trying to rip us off."

"You know, now dat you mention it, I do remember something along those lines," Big Lug said. "And I feel so terrible about it. Here, let me give ya your money back, right now. Just hand over dat ticket, and we'll call it even. Shoot, I'll even pay for them fries you just ate."

"All right!" Opera shouted as he stretched out his greasy hand to shake.

"Opera!" Wall Street grabbed his hand. "What kind of fool are you?"

Opera scrunched his eyebrows into a frown. "How many kinds are there?"

The woman saw our weakness and went for it. "And to prove there are no hard feelings, we'll even buy an extra order of fries."

I could see Opera begin to shake. The temptation must have been tremendous.

"No, Opera!" Wall Street cried. "Don't!"

Beads of perspiration broke out across his forehead as he looked from us to them . . . and from them to us. Finally, he stared down at the empty plate, its pool of grease shimmering in the light.

But the bad guys knew no shame. Big Lug raised the stakes even higher. He leaned forward and whispered, "Make that a *double* order."

It was more than Opera could handle. The poor guy's taste buds were on overload. His lips began to tremble, his face began to twitch. He gulped hard, took a deep breath, and finally asked the all-important question. "Extra crispy?"

"Stop it!" Wall Street shouted as she stepped between them. "Opera's our partner, and there's no way we're going to let you buy us out with some measly meal."

I heard Opera let out a little whimper. Poor guy.

"Well, then let me see if I can tempt you with another offer," the woman said as she pulled out a sawed-off shotgun from under her coat.

Wall Street gasped.

I groaned.

And Opera said, "I think I'd rather have the fries."

"Sorry, Tub-O," the woman hissed. "Junk food's bad for your health."

"Almost as bad as buckshot," Big Lug giggled.

"All right," Opera agreed, "I'll just have the single order then."

"The offer has expired," she growled. "And if you don't want to expire with it, I suggest you hand over that ticket."

"We don't have it," Wall Street said.

"Right," Big Lug sneered, "and I'm a monkey's uncle."

"I'm not interested in your family problems," Wall Street said. "I'm telling you the truth. We don't have the ticket on us."

"Where is it?" the woman asked. "At home?"

Wall Street's eyes lit up. The same way they do whenever she's about to make a killing off of Opera and me.

"Yeah," she nodded. "The lotto ticket's at home." She began inching toward the door. "Isn't that right, Wally?"

"Huh?"

She gave me a hard look.

"Oh yeah, right. At home." I started inching toward the door with her. "Come on, Opera," I said. "Let's go *home* and get that ticket."

"Home?" Opera said. "I thought Wally left the ticket in the—OAFF!" He would have said more, but it's hard to talk when Wall Street's elbow is jammed so hard into your stomach that it's sticking out your back. (Honestly, sometimes I think she sharpens those things.)

"So," Wall Street said as we continued easing toward the door, "why don't you two just stay here while the three of us go home, find it, and bring it right back to you."

"Not so fast!" yelled Big Lug as he blocked our way.

Uh-oh, the gig was up. He'd seen through our plan.

"If the two of us stay here and you guys go home, how uh, dat is to say, umm . . ." We watched as he struggled to think through the problem. "Uh . . ." (Amazing isn't it? How dim some folk's bulbs can glow?) Finally, he had it. "Oh yeah, if you leave and go home, how do we know you'll bring back the right ticket?"

Well, he had us there. It wasn't the right question, but it was so incredibly wrong we couldn't find an answer.

The good news was, we were just a few feet from the door. And remembering how clumsy these two were back in *My Life As Dinosaur Dental Floss,* I knew we might be able to make a run for it. I threw a glance at Wall Street. I could tell she was thinking the same thing as she threw a glance at me. Then we both threw a glance at Opera, who, unfortunately, was still throwing glances at the empty French fry plate. (I guess everyone has their priorities.)

It was now or never. Wall Street raised her leg and with one powerful

K-stomp

landed hard on top of the woman's foot.

"OW!" she cried, grabbing her foot and hopping around. "My, this is certainly a most unpleasant experience!" (Actually, that's not what she said, but since this is a G-rated book, you'll have to use your imagination.)

And, since she was having so much fun hopping on one foot, I figured the more the merrier, so I stomped down on the other:

K-stomp.

"OW! OW!" she cried. "My, this experience is even more unpleasant than the other!" The poor gal was doing more dance steps than some kid having to go to the bathroom . . . which gave us the chance to make our move.

"Let's go!" Wall Street shouted. She grabbed Opera, threw open the door, and raced outside.

"Right behind you!" I shouted as I spun around, raced toward the door, and

K-Bonk

smashed into the edge of it. I must have hit the thing pretty hard 'cause I was seeing more stars than at the Academy Awards. And what journey through unconscious-ville would be complete without a little staggering back and forth? First to the left, then to the right, then a collision with the *hopping woman.*

"Excuse me!" she cried. "If it is not an incon-

venience, would you be so kind as to release me?"
(Time for more language imagination, again.)

I would have loved to cooperate, but I was a
little busy being in a daze and hanging on to her
for dear life.

Obviously feeling left out, Big Lug got into the
act and tried to separate us. "Hey, that's my girl
you're hugging!"

Now it was an absurd kind of dance . . . the
woman hopping and yelling "Ow, ow, ow," me hanging on, and Big Lug trying to pull us apart—not,
of course, without

> *hop* "Ow!"
> *hop* "Ow!"

getting his own tootsies stomped on in the process.

But things didn't get real interesting until we
finally

> *hop, hop, hop*
> *K-Bamb!*

knocked into the table, tipped it over, and

> *K-rash!*
> *tinkle, tinkle, tinkle,*
> *glug, glug, glug. . . .*

The *K-rash* was the empty French fry plate hitting the floor. The *tinkle, tinkle, tinkle* was it turning into many pieces of French fry plate. And the *glug, glug, glug* was all that wonderful grease pouring out onto the floor.

No problem, except as we did our three-way dance it made it

> "Whoa!"
> *Slip, slip, slip*
> *K-Bamb!*

a little hard to

> "Whoa!"
> *slip, slip, slip*
> *K-Bamb!*

stand.

> *K-BAMB!*
> *K-RASH!*

That was another table biting the dust. Only this one had four empty hamburger plates on it, which meant

> *GLUG, GLUG, GLUG*

about four extra feet of grease spilling onto the floor.

"My, oh, my!" the woman cried. "That was certainly unfortunate."

I don't know how long we kept that up (it's hard to keep track of time when you keep getting knocked unconscious). But I was sure grateful when Wall Street raced back in, pulled me to my feet . . . "Come on, Wally, quit clowning around!" . . . and dragged me out the door.

K-BAMB!

Actually I would have been more grateful if she'd dragged me *out* the door instead of *into* it. But they say the third time is the charm, so after one more

K-BAMB!

into the door for old time's sake, we finally made it outside.

That was the good news. But as you know, these chapters seldom end with good news. Because back in the restaurant, staggering to their feet (and saying a few more R-rated words), our bad guys grabbed the shotgun and decided it would be great fun to begin a little chase.

Chapter 6

Returning to the Scene of the Crime

So there we were, racing for home as fast as our hot little feet could carry us. Well, at least that's where my hot little feet wanted to carry me. Unfortunately, Wall Street's feet had different ideas. When we got to the first intersection, instead of rounding the block for home, she took a right and started crossing the street.

"Where you going?" I shouted. "Home is this way!"

"I know. The zoo is this way!"

"Zoo?"

"We've got to double back!"

"Are you crazy?"

"Wally, that's where the ticket is!"

"That's also where the bad guys are!"

"We'll be on the other side of the street. We'll stay in the shadows, they'll never see us!"

"No way!" I shouted. "That's crazy talk! That's loony tunes! That's—"

"The only way to get 2.1 gazillion dollars!" she cried.

"What are we waiting for?" I shouted as I raced across the street ahead of her. "Let's get going!"

Now, I know that some of you might be thinking your ol' buddy, Wally, was having a little trouble in the greed department. Well, you're wrong, dead wrong. I wasn't having a little trouble with greed . . . I was having *a lot* of trouble with it! First, there was my destructo-zoo tour on the popcorn wagon that afternoon; then there was my minor attitude about being a hotshot before the drawing (not to speak of my major attitude after it). And now here we were starting a brand-new suicide mission. Of course, in the back of my mind, I knew it was stupid. But in the front of my mind, all I could think about was that cold, hard cash.

We managed to race across the street and duck behind a parked car just as Big Lug and the woman raced outside. By the looks of their greasy clothes, stringy hair, and the delicate sheen of oil all over their bodies, it seemed they'd managed to slip and fall on the grease-covered floor a couple hundred more times. (This would also explain why they were popping about a dozen blood vessels in anger.)

"Which way?" Big Lug yelled.

"They're heading for their homes!" the woman cried.

"Let's get 'em!"

I jumped up to start after them, but Wall Street grabbed me and pulled me back down. "Where are you going?" she whispered, "The zoo's this way."

"They're heading for our houses! We've got to warn our families."

"Let's get the ticket first."

"But—"

"Our families can take care of themselves."

"But . . . but—"

"The ticket won't."

"But . . . but . . . but—"

"And no ticket means no money."

That's when I stopped my motorboat imitation and began nodding my head in agreement. Look, I know I should have put my family first, but I figured with all that money I could buy a couple of bodyguards for them . . . shoot, I could even buy a whole army! Granted, the bad guys would probably find my house before then, but what's a minor detail like that compared to all that loot?

By now, Big Lug and the woman had disappeared around the corner. So, we got up and raced to the zoo. In less than a minute, we were standing in front of the closed ten-foot-tall gates.

"What do we do now?" Opera groaned.

"We climb over them," I said as I leaped toward the black iron bars. Unfortunately, I missed the gate by half a foot.

K-thunk!

However, I did manage to leave a lovely impression of my face on the sidewalk in front of it.

"Wally, . . ."

I rose to my feet and tried again. After all, we were talking 2.1 gazillion dollars. Besides, I knew my friends were depending on me. With great determination (and no athletic ability), I took a deep breath and started to climb the gate.

"Wally, . . ."

I continued the impossible task, working my way up the slippery bars. Minutes ticked away. It was exhausting work, but I had no choice. I couldn't let us down. Finally, I paused to catch my breath. I looked back down to check my progress. Incredibly, I was already eight, maybe even nine *inches* off the ground.

"Wally, . . ."

I pressed on, gasping for air. Nine inches . . . nine and a half. Every muscle in my body cried out in pain (and embarrassment) as I continued up and up.

"Wally!"

Finally, I looked down at my friends. No doubt they were impressed with my awesome strength. No doubt they were calling up to cheer me on. Then again, maybe it was because the gate hadn't been locked at all, and Wall Street had just pushed it open, and she was now standing inside with her hands on her hips shouting up to me: "Will you quit fooling around, Wally; we've got work to do!"

* * * * *

The zoo was scary. Without any lights and with all those unknown creatures lurking about, it was majorly creepy in a *Scream, Part XXI* kind of way.

Then there were all those strange noises—the howling hyenas, the chattering chimps, my knocking knees. It's not that I was frightened or anything, I could just think of a lot safer things I could be doing . . . like sticking my tongue into electrical outlets to see if they're on.

Still, the thought of all that money kept pushing me forward.

"ROARK! ROARK!"

"What's that?" I cried.

"Sounds like we're back at the walrus exhibit," Opera said.

I felt the rough wall beside me and stuck my head over the top. Sure enough, there was the walrus staring up at me.

"Nice boy," I whispered, "good boy."

To show his friendliness at having just been awakened, he lunged up at me with an incredible

"R O A R !"

which caused me to leap back with a terrifying

"Augh!"

which sent all of the surrounding animals into various forms of cries, screams, and screeches. The noise was awful, the sounds terrible, almost as bad as sitting through a concert of our All-School Choir. I mean, everyone was screaming at the top of their lungs. Most of all me.

"AUGH!!"

"Wally, knock it off!" Wall Street whispered.

"AUGH!"

"Wally! *Wally!!*"

"AUG—OAFF!"

Suddenly, Wall Street's elbows were back in action
. . . as pointed and painful as ever. I quit screaming and began feeling for puncture wounds.

Wall Street peered through the darkness. "The
best I figure," she said, "if this is the walrus
exhibit, then Monkey Land should be right past
the Snake Palace and over to our left."

I nodded in agreement. We continued forward
until we reached the Snake Palace. It's a pretty
cool place to visit during the day when there's lots
of light. Not so cool when there's only darkness.

"Boy, am I glad we don't have to go in there," I
said as we passed by, giving it a wide berth.

"Me, too," Wall Street agreed. "Snakes give
me the creeps."

"Not rattlesnakes," Opera argued.

"What do you mean?"

"They're supposed to be a delicacy." (Good ol'
Opera, if he can eat it, he can love it.)

"There it is! There's Monkey Land!" Wall Street
pointed across the lawn to a series of big cages,
one right next to the other. Fortunately, they were
out in the open, and the moon was full so we could
see everything. Everything including the shiny

new bars they'd just installed to replace the ones I'd busted out earlier that afternoon.

"Great," I sighed. "I can never get in there now."

"Maybe you won't have to," Wall Street said as we approached the cages.

"What do you mean?"

"Take a look." She pointed to a baby baboon sitting next to the bars. He was a real cutie with beautiful brown eyes staring out at us. But the eyes weren't nearly as beautiful as what he was gnawing on. Because there, in his hands, a little gooey from all the chewing was . . .

"The lotto ticket," Opera gasped.

"Oh, no," Wall Street groaned.

"What?" I asked.

"He's chewed off some of it."

"He what?"

"Take a look at the end. Instead of 333777, it now reads 33377."

I squinted at the ticket. Sure enough, we only had five of the winning numbers left.

Wall Street sighed sadly. "That means instead of 2.1 gazillion dollars, the ticket is only worth 2.1 million dollars."

"Great," I groaned. Still, 2.1 million dollars was better than nothing, which would explain Wall Street's next little suggestion. "Wally, see if you can reach in there and get it from him."

"Why me?" I asked.

"Why not?"

"Because."

"Because why?"

As usual her logic was flawless. I obviously had no other choice. Ever so carefully, I crawled under the iron handrail. Now came the hard part; deciding which arm to live without. If I stuck my right hand into the cage and they ripped it off, I'd have to learn to eat all over again with my left. If they ripped off my left hand, I'd have to learn to catch a baseball all over again with my right. Decisions, decisions. But, since I'd never quite mastered the fine art of catching baseballs (or doing anything else athletic, except switching channels with the remote), I figured there was really no competition.

Slowly, I shoved my left hand between the bars. Then, ever so slowlier (don't try that grammar at home, kids), I started to reach toward the baby baboon.

"Atta boy," I whispered gently. "Now, let's give Uncle Wally that nice ticket."

Baboon Baby just sat there watching quietly as my hand came closer and closer.

"Come on now," I whispered. "Here we go . . ."

But, as my hand closed in, he began to pull back.

I stretched a little farther, trying to shove my shoulder through the bars. No luck. Well, not the good kind, anyway. By the looks of things, all I'd done was manage to get myself stuck.

Uh-oh.

I tried pulling out.

Nope. I was definitely caught—squeezed in tighter than Dad trying on his old army uniform.

It was about then that I noticed Monkey Boy had begun watching my fingers. Maybe I could coax him closer. I began to wiggle them.

He leaned in to investigate.

Great, it was working. I wiggled them some more.

He bent down and started sniffing them. I wasn't sure what he thought they were, maybe midget bananas, or giant peanuts, but he definitely thought they were something to eat.

Which would explain his sudden chomping down on them with his teeth . . .

Which would explain my sudden

"AUUUUUGH!"

Which would explain his leaping back and shrieking—along with all the rest of the monkeys in the cage.

But the monkeys did more than yell. After all, someone was invading their home. It was up to every man, woman, and child to save themselves, which, unfortunately, meant destroying me. Not that they came up and physically hit me. No, this was not a ground war. Instead, it was an all-out air campaign!

FLING! FLING! FLING!

They began throwing everything that wasn't tied down—rocks, banana peels, even sand . . . and they were pretty good shots.

THUD!— "Ouch!"
SPLAT!— "Oooch!"
SPFFT! (*how else would you spell flying sand?*)—"Eeech!"

I don't know how long I stayed stuck like that doing my imitation of a human dartboard, but finally Wall Street and Opera grabbed hold of me and started to pull.

"Heave!" Wall Street shouted.

FLING! FLING! FLING!

"Ho!"

THUD! THUD! THUD!

"Heave!"

FLING! FLING! FLING!

"H—"

K-PLOP!

I popped out of the bars and tumbled to the ground on top of my buddies. A moment later, we were all scrambling for cover behind some nearby bushes.

"Wally?" Opera shouted. "Are you okay?"

"Yeah," I nodded, a little dazed as I felt for broken bones or misplaced organs. As far as I could tell, everything was all right . . . well, except for my left arm, which now dragged on the ground. (A minor side effect of being stretched two feet longer than the other.)

But Wall Street had more important things on her mind. "How are we going to get that ticket now?" she complained. "We can't reach it, and we don't have keys to get inside!"

"They don't use keys," I said.

"What?"

"It's all done electronically, with codes."

"Then we don't know the codes," she said.

Unfortunately, it was about then that my eyes landed on the main office. The one Dad and I had been in just a few hours earlier. The one where Mr. Zookeeper had unlocked the leopard cage by computer.

Now you'd think after all I'd been through, I would have kept my mouth shut. I mean, common sense said, "Admit defeat and go on home," right? Unfortunately, greed has nothing to do with common sense.

"Come on," I said, rising to my feet and starting toward the office. "I know how we can get into that cage."

Chapter 7

Breaking In

I know, breaking into the zookeeper's office wasn't like the best thing in the world to be doing; but for the past few hours I hadn't exactly been going out of my way to be doing any *best things*. In fact, as the night dragged on, I seemed to be doing more and more of the *worst things*.

To help ease my conscience, I told myself that if Mr. Zookeeper really wanted to keep people out of his office, he would have locked his windows. (I didn't bother to ask myself why he locked his doors.)

But since the windows weren't locked, I managed to climb inside and

K-Thud

fall onto the floor.

"Wally?"

"Coming," I called as I scampered back to my feet and raced to the door to unlock it.

Wall Street came bursting in, followed by Opera. "Where's this computer thingamabob?" she asked. "The one that opens the different cages?"

"Right over there." I pointed to the computer sitting on a small desk under a large bookcase. "And up there on that shelf is the notebook with all the different combinations."

"Great." She pulled up a chair, snapped on the computer, and went to work. "I'll have this puppy up and running in no time."

And she would, too. After all, computers were how she played the stock market during lunch hour at school. (And you thought I was kidding about her making her first million by fourteen.)

Meanwhile, Opera and I decided we'd kill some time by pursuing our favorite hobbies.

"Think I'll go check out the snack machines in the hall," he said.

I nodded and said, "Think I'll write some more on my superhero story."

As Opera headed into the hall, I found a tablet and a pencil. Since Wall Street was over on the computer, I figured I'd continue my story the old-fashioned way:

When we last left our handsome hero of horribly horrendous halitosis (that's a fancy word for bad breath...see how educational these stories can be?) he was about to become a billionaire...in more ways than one. Hiding behind his satellite, the dreaded and dumber-than-dirt Dollar Dude was just turning his green Megabucks beam on him.

No one's sure what made Dollar Dude so hungry for money. Some say it came when his mother accidentally left the radio turned to the stock reports all day. (Who is this Dow Jones guy, anyway?) Others insist it came after Dollar Dude won big-time in Monopoly then had his heart broken when he found out it wasn't real money.

Finally, there's the ever-popular theory that winning the lotto majorly messed up his mind. (Although, of course, we know that could never happen.)

Whatever the case, Dollar Dude loves money more than his own life...or, at least more than B.B. Boy's own life, which explains why he's turning the Megabuck beam on him.

The first thing the beam hits is our hero's feet.

B.B. Boy gasps a good-guy gasp. Already he can see his $250-a-pair high tops starting to turn green. "Please, Dollar Dude," he cries, "there's got to be a way to work this out!"

"Words are cheap," Dude hisses. "Only money talks." He gives a tiny little laugh over his tiny little joke. "So, just hold still and let me turn you into a magnificent mound of money."

Desperately, B.B. Boy tries to float to the left, but Dollar Dude keeps the beam trained on him.

Now he tries for the right.

Same beam, same story. No matter which direction our hero floats, Dollar Dude has him covered.

Soon, B.B. Boy feels a strange sensation in his feet and again looks down. Not only have his trendy tennies turned green, but his tender tootsies are turning green, too!

And then (before your tongue even has a chance to recover), his fabulous feet fully feel the ferociously felonious force.

Next come his legs. (Sorry, no L words, I wore myself out on those Ts and Fs.)

Then his waist. (Ditto with the W words.)

The point is B.B. Boy's body is turning greener than the mold on last month's spaghetti sauce. (You know, the one in the bowl shoved back in the corner of the fridge that no one ever sees?) Not only are parts of his body turning green, but they are flattening out into pieces of paper with "In God We Trust" printed all over them.

Great gobs of greenbacks! In just a matter of seconds our hero will be nothing but dollar bills. Of course, he's hoping they'll be mostly hundreds so he can buy that fancy HD TV he's had his eye on. Shoot, he'll even settle for fifties, if there are enough to—

Holy hard cash! What is he saying? The beam is obviously affecting his thinking, too.

Now his chest is turning green!

Now his neck!

In desperation, he turns to Dollar Dude. "Please, help me."

"No way," the awesomely awful and absolutely antagonistic anti-hero answers. "Soon you'll be nothing but a pile of cash. Then I'll direct my beam back to earth and

*change it all into money. And that's one
promise you can take to the bank!"*

  *His humor is obviously getting worse.
Unfortunately, so is the situation.
And then, just when you think all is lost—*

"Got it!" Wall Street exclaimed just as Opera
stepped back into the room.

I looked up from my story to see her gloating
over the computer screen.

"You say the codes are in this notebook?" she
asked, reaching for the notebook on the shelf above
her.

"That's right," I nodded. "When the guy wanted
to get into the leopard cage, the zookeeper pressed
a certain code."

Wall Street began flipping through the pages.
"Then I'm guessing each cage has a code."

"Be careful," I said as I crawled out of my chair
to join her. "We only want to unlock the monkey
cage. We don't want to unlock any of the—"

That was all I said before I realized my foot had
fallen asleep. First came the usual stumbling as
I tried to keep my balance.

"Wally, look out!"

Followed by my crashing headfirst into the book-case above the desk

K-Thud!

Followed by

K-Plop, K-Plop, K-Plop

the books falling onto the desk. Unfortunately, not all fell onto the desk. Quite a few fell on the

K-rash, K-rash, K-rash

computer.

"Wally!!"

No problem, except for the

K-rackle! K-sizzle! K-pop!

of the computer. I tell you, that baby was putting out more sparks than fireworks on the Fourth of July. Even that might have been okay, if I hadn't tried to hang on to the bookcase to keep my balance.

"Look out!" Wall Street cried. "You're pulling the whole thing down!"

I looked up just in time to see the entire bookcase, complete with its one thousand books (and its one me) tilt forward and

K-RASH!!

fall on top of the computer.

If it had sparked before, it was really going to town now.

"Look out!" Wall Street cried. "It's going to blow!"

Suddenly,

K-WOOOSH!

the computer did an Old Faithful routine.

I don't know how long it lasted. It's hard to keep track of time when you're cowering on the floor making deals with God to let you live. But when things finally quieted down, Wall Street was the first to stir. "Is everybody okay?" she asked, coughing and trying to catch her breath. "Opera?"

"Here," Opera said between coughs.

"Wally?"

"Present," I gasped.

Slowly, she rose to her feet. "Uh-oh," was all she said.

I got up and joined her. From what I could tell, I'd pretty much done the usual McDoogle remodeling job . . . which meant the place was pretty much trashed—especially the computer. It lay in a smoldering heap, sparking just a little more for old time's sake.

"It'll be okay, won't it?" I asked. "I mean, I didn't ruin anything too bad—did I?"

Wall Street said nothing. She was too busy shaking her head and marveling at my handiwork.

So was Opera.

I guess I had my answer. Well, part of it, anyway. Unfortunately, there was more to come.

"Guys?" Wall Street asked. Something outside had caught her attention and she moved to the window. "Isn't it a little weird for those kangaroos to be hopping around loose like that?"

I felt a knot in my stomach.

Opera joined her at the window and looked out. "It makes perfect sense to me," he said. The knot loosened slightly, until he finished his sentence . . . "I mean, if you're being chased by two giraffes and one polar bear, wouldn't you be hopping?"

Chapter 8

Breaking Out

I threw a look to the computer. By now it had melted down into this steaming mass of tan and yellow. (I'd say it looked exactly like my sister's famous steamed cauliflower smothered in mustard sauce, but I promised not to make fun of her cooking, so I won't.)

Suddenly, there was a loud trumpeting, and we all spun toward the window just in time to see a giant elephant lumbering past.

"Wally," Wall Street cried, "look what you've done!"

"Me?" I shouted. "You're going to blame me for this?"

Wall Street and Opera both turned to me. I knew I had to pass the blame on to someone else. I mean, that's the first rule of being a kid. And kids all around the world look up to me as their role model (now that's a scary thought). Desperately, I searched the room until I found the right excuse.

"It's not me!" I cried, pointing to the smoking pile of molten plastic. "It's that stupid computer! It's to blame!"

"Right," Wall Street said, throwing me a sarcastic look. "It's all the computer's fault."

Meanwhile, Opera had walked over to the desk for a better look. We watched as he stuck his finger into the melted goop, sniffed it, then suddenly stuck it in his mouth.

"OPERA!" I cried.

"Mmm." His eyes lit up with pleasure. "Tastes just like your sister's steamed cauliflower in mustard sauce." (Hey, he said it, not me.)

"What are we going to do?" Wall Street demanded.

"I'm not sure," I answered.

"We've got to do something!"

"How 'bout grabbing some chips," Opera suggested. "I bet this stuff makes great dip."

I ignored him and headed for the phone (or what was left of it). "We've got to call the police!" I exclaimed. "There's no other solution."

Wall Street nodded.

"What's the number for 911?" I asked.

She gave me one of her famous tell-me-you're-not-as-dumb-as-you-look looks when, suddenly, the whole office started to rattle.

"What's that?" I cried,

"Murthmuake!" Opera yelled. (He would have yelled, 'Earthquake!' but it's a little hard to yell with your mouth full of melted plastic.)

Wall Street raced back to the window to see. "No!" she shouted. "It's a stampede!"

"A what?!"

"There must be a hundred buffalo, and they're all heading for us!"

By now the entire building was shaking. Bits of plaster began falling from the ceiling, stuff was crashing to the floor.

"Hit the deck!" Wall Street shouted over the roar.

I didn't have to be told twice. Not that I had much choice. The way the ground shook, I was stumbling around hitting just about everything in the room, including the deck.

Suddenly, a window exploded. I ducked and covered my head. The shaking grew worse. Another window exploded. And another. The buffalo were on all sides of the building. Any minute I expected them to break through the walls. Someone was screaming hysterically. I knew I should shout words of encouragement and comfort to whoever it was . . . until I realized that the whoever it was was me!

I don't know how long we stayed huddled on the floor like that, but eventually things started to quiet down. Until, finally, it was over.

Slowly, I lifted my head. The good news was, the walls were still standing. The bad news was, they were about the only things standing. Every picture, every book, everything else lay broken and shattered on the floor.

With the greatest effort I staggered to my feet. As far as I could tell most of my bones were unbroken, and the majority of my internal organs were still in place. Wall Street was also getting up, dusting herself off and shaking plaster out of her hair.

"Where's Opera?" I asked.

She looked around the ruins, then shrugged.

"Opera?" I called. "Opera, where are you?"

No answer.

"Opera?" Wall Street yelled. She began moving stuff around. "Opera, can you hear me?"

"Opera?" I didn't want to panic, but the guy wasn't answering. "Opera, are you all right?" Still nothing. I began pushing some junk aside looking for him. "Opera?"

"Opera, answer me!" I could tell by the tone of Wall Street's voice that she was starting to get scared, too. "Opera!"

We had to find him. If he was buried, we had to

pull him out. If he was hurt, we had to get him to the hospital. I started digging more frantically, pushing and shoving more and more stuff out of the way "Opera! Opera!" We'd been best friends as long as I could remember. "Opera!" If something happened to him, I could never forgive myself. "Opera?"

Wall Street was shouting, too. "Opera! Opera!"

How could this have happened? How could my best friend have gotten hurt just because of some stupid lotto ticket? Just because we wanted to be rich? "Opera!" What had Mom said? *"I've seen too many lives ruined over greed."* Was this one of them? Could I have lost my very best friend just because of—

"He's over here!" Wall Street shouted from the other side of the room.

I raced over the piles of junk.

"Help me push this filing cabinet off of him," Wall Street yelled.

I nodded, and with all of our effort (well, mostly with all of Wall Street's effort), we managed to slide the thing off Opera and onto the floor.

He let out a slight groan.

"Opera!" I shouted. "Opera. can you hear me?"

"Opera!" Wall Street yelled. By now we were both on our knees beside him. "Opera!"

That's when his eyes fluttered, then finally opened.

A wave of relief washed over me. "Opera," I cried, "are you all right?"

He slowly nodded.

"Say something," Wall Street urged. "Can you talk? Tell us how you feel!"

With the greatest effort, he started to part his lips.

"Are you okay?" I asked. "Where does it hurt?"

"Come on, Opera," Wall Street demanded, "say something to us!"

Then, with a faint smile crossing his face, he finally opened his mouth, and let out the world's longest and biggest

"B U R P!"

* * * * *

That little scare really shook me up. And it really got me to thinking about what Mom had said about loving money—about all the crazy things loving it makes people do . . . about all the crazy things it was making *me* do. Maybe she was right, maybe it would have been better if we had never won the Gazillion Dollar Lotto. I looked around the destroyed office and let out a long sigh. Well, at least we were safe in here. The animals could be roaming outside all they wanted, but as

long as we stayed inside until daybreak and until
we were rescued, we'd be just—

"Wally?"

I looked over at Wall Street. She was standing
near a window . . . or at least where a window had
been.

"Take a look at this," she said.

I made my way through the broken glass, the
broken office equipment, the broken everything.
Once I was beside her, she quietly pointed outside.
There, just a few yards away and sitting on a
bench, was my cute little Baboon Baby. More
important, in Baboon Baby's hand was the lotto
ticket—or what was left of it.

"Do you see what I see?" Wall Street asked.

"I'm afraid so," I sighed.

By the looks of things the little critter had
gnawed off more of the ticket—another one of the
sevens was missing, which meant we only had
four of the six winning numbers left. Now our 2.1
gazillion dollars, which had been reduced to 2.1
million, was only worth 2.1 thousand dollars.

Still, 2.1 thousand was better than 2.1 nothing.

I know we should have stayed in the building
where it was nice and safe. Inside, where there
were no running elephants, no lumbering polar
bears, and no stampeding buffalo. Unfortunately,
inside there was also no 2.1 thousand dollars.

"So what are we waiting for?" Wall Street asked.

"I don't know," I hesitated. "I mean things have really gotten out of hand . . ."

"Wally, the ticket's right out there. All we have to do is go outside and grab it!"

"I know, but . . . look at all we've destroyed."

"Exactly," she nodded. "We've ruined everything we can possibly ruin. Nothing more can go wrong. Now all we have to do is get our hands on that ticket and the money will be ours."

I was starting to weaken, and she could see it.

"Think of it, Wally, . . . 2.1 thousand dollars. Do you have any idea what you could buy with that?"

She was right, of course. 2.1 thousand was still a fortune. Even split three ways, there was no telling what all I could buy with it. Yes sir, the ol' greed was already starting to return. I knew it was time to fight it, time to take a stand, time to resist temptation and be a real man.

"So what are we waiting for?" I said. (So much for my manhood.)

"I'm with you," Wall Street grinned.

"Can we take what's left of the computer along in case we get hungry?" Opera asked.

With more than the usual amount of guilt, I joined my friends as we climbed over the remains of the office and finally made it outside. Actually, I wasn't feeling too bad . . . because the more I thought of all that money, the more Mom's voice seemed to fade from my memory.

Outside, it was sort of like the Garden of Eden, with all the flying parrots, crawling tortoises, antelopes, and everything. I figured as long as we kept our eyes open for any of the bigger animals, especially the meat-eating kind with sharp claws and even sharper teeth, we'd probably be okay.

There was, however, one type of animal we hadn't counted on:

click-click.

"Hold it right there, kiddies."

The two-legged kind with sawed-off shotguns.

"Turn around nice and slow."

All three of us obeyed until we were facing our old pals, Big Lug and his girlfriend. They looked pretty mad. Add to that their greasy bodies, stringy hair, torn and shredded clothing (I guess surviving a buffalo stampede will do that to a person), and you get your basic unhappy bad guys.

"Now, where's da ticket?" Big Lug growled.

"We don't have it!" Wall Street answered.

"You know," the woman said, waving her rifle at us, "I'm getting real tired of that excuse."

"Yeah," Big Lug agreed. "Can't you think up another?"

"Honest," Opera said, "we don't have it."

"Then where is it?" the woman demanded.

"There," Opera pointed to Baboon Baby sitting on a nearby bench. By now he'd gnawed off all of the sevens and there were only three of the threes left. (Guess that made it 2.1 hundred dollars.)

The woman gasped. Big Lug gasped! And the three of us just sort of groaned and rolled our eyes.

Then, without a word, the woman lunged toward the baboon. The little guy screamed, leaped off the bench, and scampered around a hedge. We followed, but didn't get too awfully far before we ran into . . . Mama Baboon. She was a huge animal. She clung to Baby Baboon with one hand and bared her fangs at us ferociously. Before we had a chance to introduce ourselves, she let out an unearthly howl that grew into a chilling scream. I wasn't sure what she was saying, but by the way a dozen other angry monkeys and ape types came running to her side, I figured it wasn't your typical, "How do you do?"

It only took a second for us to see what incredible danger we were in. And less than that for us to spin around and start running for our lives. But, believing in the old saying, "Monkey see, monkey do," the rest of the apes did the same . . . they took off running for our lives, too!

"Oo-oo ah-ah ee-ee!"

What they were going to do when they caught us was beyond me, but I wasn't sticking around to find out.

So there we were, five humans merrily jogging through the zoo followed by a dozen cute baboons, orangutans, and what looked like a couple of gorillas.

A couple of gorillas!!

So, there we were, five humans racing for all we were worth through the zoo, desperately trying to escape the killer apes.

We had to get away; we had to hide. Since I was in the lead (being the world's greatest chicken also makes you the world's fastest runner), I was the one who spotted the building we were fast approaching. "In here!" I shouted. "Let's hide in here!"

Unfortunately, "in here" just happened to be the Snake Palace.

Unfortunatelier, (there's that "word" again) no one bothered to question my wisdom. Well, no one but the apes who decided to stay outside. (Obviously, they knew something we didn't.)

Like I said before, the Snake Palace is a neat place to visit in the daytime. You get to walk on a ramp just a few feet over a swarming snake pit, and you get to check out all the cool spiders and giant cockroaches in glass cases on each side—not to mention all the slithering lizards and other ultra-cool crawly things. At least they're ultra-cool when they're locked up and out of reach. They're not so cool when they've been unlocked and are swarming all around your feet.

Especially if your feet are world famous for their klutziness.

The good news was, we made it about halfway through the Snake Palace before I finally tripped and fell. The bad news was, *half*way is not the same as *all* the way. The badder news was that I was still in the lead. The baddest news was that when I fell,

"Oaff!"

everyone else fell, too.

"Oaff!"
"Oaff!"
"Oaff!"
"Oaff!"

So there I was, lying face down on the ramp, with more people piled on top of me than an NFL quarterback on a bad day. It was a little freaky opening my eyes and seeing the snake pit with all the hissing, slithering bodies just a few feet below me. But that wasn't nearly as bad as when I finally looked up and noticed I was face-to-face with a giant . . . hairy . . . tarantula!

Now I had two choices. Be cool and watch as its hairy legs crawled onto my chin, dragging its creepy body across my mouth, and over my face . . . or be real and scream like a madman.

Being the down-to-earth kind of guy I am, I knew I didn't really have a choice. I opened my mouth and:

"Augh!"

What on earth was that? I tried again:

"Augh!"

I guess with so many people on top of me that's all I could squeeze out.

I watched in horror as Harry the Tarantula approached—his beady little eyes, not to mention his megasize mouth, crawling closer and closer to my own.

I figured now was as good a time as any to freak out. In sheer terror, I bucked and squirmed and twisted. Then I twisted and squirmed and bucked.

Wall Street and Opera managed to hang on.

Unfortunately, the woman and Big Lug did not. With more than the daily recommended amount of screaming (and words my G-rated fingers can't type) they not only rolled off of me . . . but they rolled off of the ramp. No problem, except as I said, we were directly over the snake pit.

Well, Wall Street, Opera, and I were directly over the snake pit. The woman and Big Lug were now directly in the middle of it!

It was pretty creepy seeing the things slithering and crawling all over them . . . watching as a thousand tongues flickered in and out, licking the grease off their clothes, their faces, their hair. I suppose the two should have been grateful they were finally getting cleaned up—though I bet they would have preferred a good, hot shower, instead.

"Come on!" Wall Street grabbed my hand. "Let's get out of here!" She pulled me up, and the three of us started to run out of the place.

Part of me wanted to stay and help, but with my birthday just around the corner and knowing how hard it is for dead people to unwrap presents, I decided to keep running.

"What about the bad guys?" Opera cried.

"They'll be okay," Wall Street shouted as we finally stumbled out into the moonlight. "None of the snakes are poisonous, and they've all been defanged."

"That's great," I said as I stood there trying to

catch my breath. "I just wish they would have defanged the mountain lions."

"Defang mountain lions?" Wall Street scoffed. "Why would you want them to do that?"

"MROWWWwww!"

I raised my hand and pointed. Less than ten feet away, crouched and ready to attack, was a fierce (and I'm guessing pretty hungry) mountain lion.

Unfortunately, that wasn't the only surprise . . .

Because, suddenly, we were bathed in a blinding white light. Then, overhead we heard

whop-whop-whop-whop.

We looked up to see a giant helicopter directly overhead. It was hard to make out the details because of the glaring light, but the best I could see, they had about a hundred SWAT-type guys leaning out, all aiming rifles at us. Then there was the little warning someone was shouting through a loudspeaker:

"THIS IS THE MIDDLETOWN POLICE. DON'T MOVE OR WE WILL OPEN FIRE."

Don't get me wrong, I was all in favor of not moving, especially if it meant another problem in unwrapping those birthday gifts we just talked about. But I had one minor problem:

"MROWWWwww . . ."

By the looks of things Ol' Sylvester, perched on that rock, was just about to turn us all into cat chow.

"Nice kitty, kitty, kitty," I called, giving him a friendly little wave.

Apparently the SWAT boys didn't like my friendliness because, suddenly, a dozen little laser lights focused on my body. I was covered with more red dots than my brother's face on a bad acne day.

"WE SAID, DON'T MOVE!"

"MROWWWwww . . ."

"All right," I whispered to the others. "If anybody's got some ideas, I'm open to suggestions."

Chapter 9

Just Like Old Times

So, there I was trying to decide whether I wanted to become human cat food or SWAT Swiss cheese when, all of the sudden, Big Lug and his lady friend came staggering out of the Snake Palace. With the thousand snakes swarming all over them! I guessed they weren't having the best of times . . . and by the way the woman kept screaming and waving around her shotgun I guess I had guessed the right guess.

Unfortunately for her, nothing attracts a SWAT team's attention like a crazed person waving around a shotgun. Before I knew it, all my little red laser pals had migrated over to the woman. Now, my only worry was the growling mountain lion and . . . oh, yeah,

"Oo-oo ah-ah ee-ee!"

those dozen ape types who had just circled

around the Snake Palace and were now charging at us.

I looked at Wall Street and Opera. Wall Street and Opera looked at me. And then we all did what we all do best. We screamed our lungs out!

The sound of hysterically screaming kids was new to Ol' Puss 'n' Boots and for a second he drew back in fear. But a second was all we needed. The three of us took off running faster than Mom runs up credit card charges at Christmas.

The good news was, we were running fast. The bad news was that we were surrounded and had no place to run fast to . . . which is almost the same as not running at all . . . unless you count all of our running back and forth into one another:

> *K-Bang*—"Ow!"
> *K-Bamb*—"Sorry!"
> *K-Bop*—"Watch it!"

To our left was the Snake Palace, to our right was the mountain lion, and racing directly at us were the monkeys—who by now were (get ready) . . . really going *ape* over us. (Hey, I warned you.)

Unfortunately, it was about this time that I noticed an escape route. "Up there!" I shouted. "In the tree!"

"What?" Wall Street cried.

"Let's climb that tree! Hurry, we don't have much time!"

Quicker than you can say, "Hey, wait a minute, don't mountain lions also climb trees? And what about monkeys, don't they climb trees, too? And what about the SWAT helicopter—if we climb the tree aren't we just getting closer to all those guys with all those guns who can—"

(All right, all right, I get the picture!)

The point is, we were in too much of a hurry to think through those tiny details. And since you didn't happen to be around to offer all of that swell advice, we just sort of kept climbing higher and higher and higher some more.

"Say, Opera?" I finally heard Wall Street ask from behind me. "Your breath stinks. Have you been eating raw meat again?"

"Not me," Opera said. "It's that person behind me."

"There's nobody behind you."

"MROWWWwww . . ."

"There is now," Opera shouted. "CLIMB!"

I threw a look over my shoulder, and sure enough, directly behind Opera was the big cat . . . and directly behind the big cat (in case he felt like leaving leftovers) were the . . .

"Oo-oo ah-ah ee-ee!"

big apes.

Things did not look good. Unfortunately, they were about to look a lot worse. It seemed the higher we climbed, the skinnier the tree got . . . and the skinnier the tree got the less it could hold our weight. Until . . .

CRACK

the top broke off, which led to your standard

"AUGHHHhhh . . ."

that was followed by

K-CRASH

tumble, "Ouch!" *tumble,* "Ooch!" *tumble,* "Eech!"

"YEEEEEOW. . . ."

Let's see if I can sort out the details for you. The "AUGHHHhhh . . ." was us falling, the *K-CRASH* was us hitting the ground, the *tumble* "Ouch, ooch, eech" was me rolling away from my friends and down the world's steepest ridge, which quickly turned into the world's steepest cliff, and that should explain the "YEEEEEOW!"

Unfortunately, there was one more sound effect left to come:

K-SMRUNCH!

If the noise sounds strange, it should. That's the sound of one very bruised boy landing on the back of one very startled giraffe. And the interesting thing about giraffes is that when they are startled they run!

"H-h-help!" I screamed, bouncing up and down on its bony back. "Wh-ere-ere . . . are-re-re . . . the brak-ak-akes . . . on this thing-ing-ing!"

But of course there were no brakes, which explains why we kept running. That, and the fact that

whop-whop-whop-whop

the boys in the SWAT helicopter were scaring him. They obviously thought I was trying to get away and started chasing us.

"THIS IS THE MIDDLETOWN POLICE!" they shouted. "CEASE AND DESIST! CEASE AND DESIST!"

I had no idea who 'Cease or Desist' were, but I did recognize my old friends the red laser dots when they reappeared on my jacket for a little reunion. Of course, the helicopter only frightened the giraffe more, making him run harder and faster, which only made me bounce hard-er-er-er and fast-er-er-er, until one bounce was just a little too hard, sending me just a little too high, as he continued running just a little too fast.

Translation: By the time I finally came back down, my giraffe friend was long gone.

Unfortunately, he may have been gone, but

K-CRASH!

my old pal, the popcorn wagon, wasn't. I landed directly on top of it. I suppose I should have been impressed that Mr. Zookeeper had fixed it so quickly. I would have been more impressed if he hadn't put newer and faster wheels on it, which meant

Roll . . . roll . . . roll, roll, rollrollrollrollroll . . .

I picked up a lot of speed . . . *fast.*

So there I was, right back where I started from . . . except I was a little higher up on the hill and going a lot faster. No problem, except for the poor unsuspecting animals who didn't see me coming:

"Baaaa"—K-Bamb!
"Roarrr" —K-Bump!
"Cock-a-doodle"—K-Bounce!

But, in spite of all the flying fur and feathers, I
was able to look ahead and spot my old buddy . . .
Baby Baboon. He was sitting on a rock not too far
ahead . . . and he was still holding the lotto ticket!
It looked a lot gooier and smaller (which probably
meant it was now down to 2.1 dollars) but it made
no difference. It was still mine, and I was going
to get it.

The wagon continued racing toward him.
I leaned out, stretching for all I was worth.
The wagon was nearly there.
I leaned a little farther.
There was his hand . . . there was my ticket . . .
I leaned just a little farther until, finally:

K-SNATCH!

I got it! I got the lotto ticket! Victory was mine!
Of course, it would have been more of a victory if I'd
had time to celebrate. But it's hard to celebrate when

K-SMASH!!!

your popcorn wagon has just hit the wall of the walrus exhibit. Even that wouldn't have been so bad if I would have stopped with it.

But, of course, I didn't. I just kept on sailing, right over the wall, right over the little walrus lake, and right into a giant boulder.

> *(Sorry, no sound effects. It's hard to remember sound effects when you've been knocked totally unconscious.)*

Unfortunately, being totally unconscious is not the same as being totally dead. Which meant I eventually had to wake up. I gave a few groans, rolled over, and slowly opened my eyes.

I wished I hadn't.

Because there, staring down at me from a rock ledge, was the giant walrus. I couldn't tell if he was glad for my little visit or not, but I figured it wouldn't hurt to turn on the McDoogle charm just in case he was still a little cranky.

"Nice boy," I muttered, trying to sit up. "Good fellow."

He tilted his head at me quizzically.

"You're a nice walrus, aren't you?"

He snorted loudly . . .

. . . which made me jump,

. . . which made him jump,

. . . which made me cry out,

. . . which made him jump even more.

The good news was that I had finally discovered a creature who was even more clumsy than myself. The bad news was that when that creature slipped off the ledge, he had no place to fall but directly on top of

"OAFF!"

me.

So there I lay under 3,000 pounds of muscle and blubber, squished flatter than a pancake smashed by a sumo wrestler driving a semi. It was awful, terrible, almost as bad as the time Opera fell on me. (Who knows, maybe the two are distant relatives.) But the fun and games weren't entirely over. Because, once again I heard

whop-whop-whop-whop—

the SWAT team approaching overhead. This time, however, they didn't say anything. I guess it's hard to talk when you can't stop laughing. Besides, what did they have to worry about? It wasn't like I was going anywhere. I couldn't move until the walrus moved. In fact, I could barely breathe. All I could do was just lie there, like some giant walrus whoopee cushion, trying to figure out how I'd gotten into this mess . . . though I suspected a lot of it had to do with that one tiny word whose spelling begins with *GR,* ends with *EED.*

Once again I thought of Mom's words, and once again I felt pretty stupid. Sure, I still had the lotto ticket, it was right there in my hand . . . at least what was left of it. But I would have given it away, even if it had all of its numbers, to avoid what I'd been through these last forty-eight hours.

I glanced over to my hand and turned the ticket around, just to see if there were any numbers left. Unfortunately, that was all the movement necessary to catch Ol' Waldo the Walrus's attention. The creature tilted his head and then in one swift movement, dropped his neck, wrapped his lips around the ticket, and sucked it into his mouth like a giant vacuum cleaner!

I couldn't believe it. One minute it was there, the next it was gone. Just like that. Now there was nothing left of the lucky lotto ticket. Nothing at all. Well, nothing except for one very loud and rather obnoxious

"BURP!"

Hmm . . . maybe he really is related to Opera.

Chapter 10

Wrapping Up

For the most part, Mr. Zookeeper was pretty cool about all the damage we did to his place. I mean it wasn't like he was jumping up and down or screaming or pulling out his hair . . . at least not since he'd been heavily tranquilized and wrapped in a straitjacket.

Unfortunately, Dad didn't take it quite so well. The best I figure, he was on his second or third heart attack when the SWAT team finally got around to handing me over to him. (They must have figured his punishment would be worse than anything they could throw at me. And this time, they'd finally figured right.)

At the moment Dad was deep into Phase One of the punishment . . .

The Lecture:

This is where he paces back and forth, shaking

his head and saying things like, "What could you have possibly been thinking?"

"The lotto ticket," I mumbled.

"What could have made you so stupid?" he demanded.

"The lotto ticket."

"What on earth possessed you?"

"The lotto ticket."

We would have gone on like that for hours if we hadn't been interrupted by the police. They were leading Big Lug and the woman past us to some police cars. I wanted to wish them luck and tell them there were no hard feelings, but it didn't look like they could hear.

Big Lug was too busy slapping at imaginary snakes crawling all over his body and screaming, "Get 'em off! Get 'em off! Somebody get 'em off!"

And the woman, who was wearing the same dazed expression as Mr. Zookeeper (without the help of the tranquilizer), had definitely blown a mental circuit or two. You could tell by her mindless grin and her even more mindless singing, "La-la-la-la-la-la . . ."

We watched as they were loaded into the cars. Then Dad turned to me and began Phase Two of the punishment . . .

The Sentencing:

"We've got to make sure this doesn't happen again. You've got to learn from your mistakes."

I wanted to tell him that I'd already learned, plenty—especially when it came to greed. But I figured it was best to lie low in case he tried to go *interactive* on me. You know, *interactive*—that's when your parents ask *you* what punishment you think you should have? (Personally, I think such questions should be outlawed as cruel and unusual punishment. I mean, if we go to all of the bother of getting into trouble, the least they can do is figure out how to punish us.) But not Dad.

"So, tell me," he asked as we climbed into the family van, "what do you think your punishment should be?"

Desperately, I tried to think up something that would be terrible, something that would be horrible, something that would make a lasting impression on me for the rest of my life. There was only one thing that could be so awful . . .

"Make me buy another lotto ticket?" I offered.

He gave me one of those Dad scowls. You know, the type that makes you want to crawl under the seat in your best Wicked-Witch-of-the-West-Meets a-Bucket-of-Water routine. But instead of yelling or anything, he simply said, "I think you better think again."

I scrunched my forehead into a frown but no answer came.

"Well, you give it some thought," Dad said as he started up the van. "Right now, I better get you home. Your sister's waiting with a wonderful dessert she's made up just for you."

"That's it!" I shouted. "That could be my punishment. Make me eat it!"

For the briefest second Dad almost smiled, then he caught himself and tried to look serious. "No, son," he said. "Think of something else."

"What if I ask for seconds?"

"Wallace."

I sighed heavily and looked out the window. The van slowly pulled away. Off in the distance I could see Wall Street and Opera having similar conversations with their parents. Yes sir, things had not gone well. Not well at all. But, at least it was over. Well, all except for the punishment.

As I rode along, I let my mind drift back to B.B. Boy and Dollar Dude. Sometimes working on stories clears my mind and helps me think better. Let's see, where were we . . .

When we last left our brilliantly brave, but badly beaten up, B.B. Boy, he was about to come into a lot of

money...actually, he was about to become
a lot of money. Fives, tens, twenties,
you name it, he was becoming it. And not
those cool old-fashioned bills either,
but those new, weird-looking ones. All
thanks to Dollar Dude and his not-so-
magnificent Megabuck Beam.

"Why?" our hero gasps as he floats in
the center of the ghastly green beam.
"Why is turning everything into money
so important to you?"

"Because, B.B. Brain, money is what
makes people happy."

"Do you...really..." It's becoming
harder for our hero to talk. Already his
lips have turned green and his face
shows the outlines of all those balding
old-timers who used to be our presi-
dents. "Do you really believe...money
is what makes people...happy?"

"Of course," the Dude answers. "As a
bad guy, I'm supposed to believe that
kind of stuff."

"But what about love..." our hero
gasps, "and people, and friends?"

"Oh, no!" the boisterous bad boy bellows.
"Are we already coming to the moral of
this story?"

"I'm afraid so," our hero answers, although it's getting harder to understand his words since his teeth and tongue are also turning into paper ...another good reason to hurry and get to the moral.

Speaking of morals, here it comes: "Don't you see..." our hero gasps, "loving money...only leads to...trouble." By now his voice is barely above a whisper.

"Oh, yeah?" Dude demands. "And just what makes you so smart?"

"I'm not...but our author is."

"And how does he know?"

"Last forty-eight hours...he spent ...making the same mistakes."

"No way!"

"Way..." our hero gasps. "Why else do we have to wait...all this time ...between our scenes?" But that's all he can say. Now there's only the dry crackle of dollar bills.

Oh, no! It's too late! B.B. Boy has completely turned into a lump of loot, a mound of money, a clod of cash. Our story is over. There will be no more lecturing on the evils of loving money.

But, fortunately, Dollar Dude wants to
hear more (whew, that was close). With
one swift move, he reaches for the
reverse switch. Quicker than you can
say, "Hey, wait a minute, isn't this
just a little too convenient?" the
effects of the machine start to reverse.
Soon B.B. Boy's tongue is a real tongue
again, his lips are real lips again, his
breath...well, it can still stop a mule
at twenty paces.

"Please," Dollar Dude begs, being
careful to avoid B.B. Boy's breath.
"Tell me more about this author of ours.
If I can learn from his mistakes, maybe
I won't make them myself."

"Mistakes," B.B. Boy chuckles. "If you
want mistakes, he's your man. In fact,
as far as I can tell, he's made every
mistake known to the human race...and
invented a few new ones along the way.
He's even written a whole series of
books about them."

"Really?"

"Absolutely. Hey, I have a neato-
keen idea. Why don't you come on down to
my house, and I'll loan you a couple
of them?"

"You'd do that for me? Loan me the books?"

"Sure, that way you won't have to buy them...(but don't tell our author friend, he's sort of sensitive to that kind of stuff. Just look back on page 38)."

"Well," Dollar Dude grins, "that's a spiffy swell idea. Thanks, B.B. Boy."

"Don't mention it," B.B. Boy smiles, "...especially to the author."

And so together, arm in arm, the two conveniently catch the Space Shuttle on its way back to earth as the Megabeam continues reversing its effects, changing those tons of twenties back into buildings, those towers of tens back into light poles, and those mounds of fluffy five-dollar bills back into those strange-looking VW Beetles. (Hey, two out of three isn't bad!)

I continued staring out the window thinking about the ending of my story. I don't want to say it was too sweet or sugary, but the next time you go to the dentist and he discovers a half-dozen cavities, you'll know who is to blame.

Still, it doesn't hurt to bring some happiness into the world. And if people can learn from all of my mishaps, so much the better. Because, as far as I can tell, it will be a long, long time before they come to an end.

You'll want to read them all.

THE INCREDIBLE WORLDS OF WALLY McDOOGLE

#1—*My Life As a Smashed Burrito with Extra Hot Sauce*
Twelve-year-old Wally—"The walking disaster area"—is forced to stand up to Camp Wahkah Wahkah's number one all-American bad guy. One hilarious mishap follows another until, fighting together for their very lives, Wally learns the need for even his worst enemy to receive Jesus Christ.
(ISBN 0-8499-3402-8)

#2—*My Life As Alien Monster Bait*
"Hollyweird" comes to Middletown! Wally's a superstar! A movie company has chosen our hero to be eaten by their mechanical "Mutant from Mars!" It's a close race as to which will consume Wally first—the disaster-plagued special effects "monster" or his own out-of-control pride . . . until he learns the cost of true friendship and of God's command for humility.
(ISBN 0-8499-3403-6)

#3—*My Life As a Broken Bungee Cord*
A hot-air balloon race! What could be more fun? Then again, we're talking about Wally McDoogle, the "Human Catastrophe." Calamity builds on calamity until, with his life on the line, Wally learns what it means to FULLY put his trust in God.
(ISBN 0-8499-3404-4)

#4—*My Life As Crocodile Junk Food*
Wally visits missionary friends in the South American rain forest. Here he stumbles onto a whole new set of impossible predicaments . . . until he understands the need and joy of sharing Jesus Christ with others. (ISBN 0-8499-3405-2)

#5—*My Life As Dinosaur Dental Floss*
It starts with a practical joke that snowballs into near disaster. Risking his life to protect his country, Wally is pursued by a

SWAT team, bungling terrorists, photosnapping tourists, Gary the Gorilla, and a TV news reporter. After prehistoric-size mishaps and a talk with the President, Wally learns that maybe honesty really is the best policy.
(ISBN 0-8499-3537-7)

#6—My Life As a Torpedo Test Target

Wally uncovers the mysterious secrets of a sunken submarine. As dreams of fame and glory increase, so do the famous McDoogle mishaps. Besides hostile sea creatures, hostile pirates, and hostile Wally McDoogle clumsiness, there is the war against his own greed and selfishness. It isn't until Wally finds himself on a wild ride atop a misguided torpedo that he realizes the source of true greatness.
(ISBN 0-8499-3538-5)

#7—My Life As a Human Hockey Puck

Look out . . . Wally McDoogle turns athlete! Jealousy and envy drive Wally from one hilarious calamity to another until, as the team's mascot, he learns humility while suddenly being thrown in to play goalie for the Middletown Super Chickens! (ISBN 0-8499-3601-2)

#8—My Life As an Afterthought Astronaut

"Just cause I didn't follow the rules doesn't make it my fault that the Space Shuttle almost crashed. Well, okay, maybe it was sort of my fault. But not the part when Pilot O'Brien was spacewalking and I accidently knocked him halfway to Jupiter. . . ." So begins another hilarious Wally McDoogle MISadventure as our boy blunder stows aboard the Space Shuttle and learns the importance of: Obeying the Rules!
(ISBN 0-8499-3602-0)

#9—My Life As Reindeer Road Kill

Santa on an out-of-control four wheeler? Electrical Rudolph on the rampage? Nothing unusual, just Wally McDoogle doing some last-minute Christmas shopping . . . FOR GOD! Our boy blunder dreams that an angel has invited him to a birthday party for Jesus. Chaos and comedy follow as he turns the town upside down looking for the perfect gift, until he finally bumbles his way into the real reason for the Season. (ISBN 0-8499-3866-X)